WHAT IS BIT

It's a book series for Young Adult and
theatre-lovers, as well as a blog at www
page with loads of costume, make-up, set and prop ideas for your next
show.

WHAT ARE PEOPLE SAYING ABOUT BIT PLAYERS?

"I loved that the author captured the sights, sounds, and feel of the
theatre. The characters are interesting and I became invested in them.
The best friends, one changing, are classic and most middle school kids
will identify with them. It felt real. The song parodies were amazing. I
worked with a comedy troupe that did song parodies and these were
spot on! I loved that Ms. Stevens recommends that you pull up the
original songs on your computer, then you can sing along. They were
'brilliant'. This was a very well written novel. I enjoyed it!"

-- Writer's Digest Self-Published Book Award Judge

"The story is wonderful. It's nice to read a book geared towards young
adults that isn't full of sex and murder. There's mystery, romance, and
theatre! How could you go wrong? I especially loved singing along
throughout the book. Wonderful! I would definitely recommend it to
young adults."

-- Morgan Smith, Board Member, Imagine That! Theatre

"The characters in Bit Players were well developed three-dimensional
people I cared more and more about as I read this novel. The teen
voices struck just the right chord and the issues all high school juniors
and seniors deal with were mentioned but not dwelt upon. This was a
fun read, I could not wait to see what happened next...I will definitely
add it to my YA collection."

-- Kathy J. Stevens MLIS, Youth Services Librarian, Baxter Memorial Library

"The pursuit of fame starts young. *Bit Players, Has-Been Actors, and Other Posers* is based on the high school drama we all have faced at some level or another. Sadie Perkins quests to rise up and gain a bit more of that high school fame, and she struggles to even get the show off the ground during a tumultuous time. *Bit Players, Has-Been Actors, and Other Posers* is a riveting and much recommended pick for any young adult fiction collection.

-- *Midwest Book Review*

Readers rate the books 4.5 to 5 stars on Amazon. Some reader reviews:

"Stevens' stories are much better written and are more engaging than the popular vampire series of wishy-washy twilight characters. If you're in High School or if your kid is, the Bit Players series is the better choice by far."

"The second book in the Bit Players series is great! Like the first book, it entwines a plot of mystery and romance around the production of an original musical/play...I thought the connection between the bullying in the "real life" of the characters and its portrayal in the musical they were producing was brilliant and very relevant in today's world. Stevens tackles tough topics such as bullying and sexual orientation with finesse and without preaching to the readers. She presents these topics not only from the point of view of the student, but also the opinions (right or wrong) of teachers, parents and strangers...I hope that some day the original musical in this book makes it to our local stage."

"I did high school theatre and this book took me right back to how that all felt – the friendships, the politics, the thrill of being in a show. It was cool how the book included modern songs but with new lyrics. I really liked the lead character Sadie, in the end. At first I wasn't sure, but I guess that's what makes her a good character, that she's not perfect. And I was totally intrigued wondering who the bully was. All in all, a really fun read!"

"The characters were well developed and there were plot twists and surprises you don't see coming. I could easily see this becoming a movie. A great read!"

"This was so entertaining. It reads just like a script, and includes links to music that go with the book. Read this in one sitting! This would be a great book to use as a guide for high school theatre teachers; maybe they could use the story and get ideas for their own plays or just let the students read this and have discussions. I think young readers can relate to this story whether they are in theater or not – friends, bullies, and making it to the end of high school, makes for a good story along with the play and music." *(from Goodreads)*

"To my surprise (since I'm a "sports dad" and not a theater-guy) I loved this book. It was an easy read and I really liked the characters and the story moved right along. Our family never got involved with the *Twilight* stuff, so I thought I'd be missing a lot of references or inside information, but that wasn't the case. The biggest compliment I can give is I found myself disappointed when my train arrived at the station, as I'd have to stop reading until my next commute!"

"I really like this book. The teens are so much like kids at my school that they seem like real friends, and I want to know them even better. I hope the author writes a sequel to Bit Players. I love the theater, especially musicals, and there aren't many books on that subject. The plot moves fast, and it's a fun read."

"S.M. Stevens did an excellent job creating the characters and developing the story of a high school drama production. Although I have never watched *Glee* or *Twilight*, I was captivated by the writing style and anxiously reading to find out what happened next. It is a fun, easy-reading story with a surprising plot twist at the end. I know many of my students will love to read this story. I am looking forward to the next "production"!

BIT PLAYERS, BIRD GIRLS AND FAKE BREAK-UPS

S.M. Stevens

Lizzy,

Enjoy - I love
your blog!

S.M. Stevens

This is a work of fiction. Any resemblance to actual events, locales or persons, living or dead, is entirely coincidental.

Dedicated to Walter Stump and
to Sarah Richards and Avi Wolf,
for instilling in me and those closest to me
a passion for theatre that will last a lifetime.

To match up the songs in this book with the
YouTube versions they were based on, go to:
www.BitPlayers.me/videos/bp3.

CHAPTER 1: DR. WHO?

THE SADIE AND ALEX REUNION

EXT. OUTSIDE ALEX'S HOUSE - DAY

The torn screen door with the peeling-paint frame flies open, revealing ALEX HOLMAN inside his home.

SADIE PERKINS run-walks up the path to Alex's front door, ten torturous steps away, her long, light auburn hair - perfectly curled for once - bouncing against her back. Her expression alternates between anticipation and apprehension, a teen angst version of the comedy and tragedy theatre masks.

Unable to wait, Alex pushes the screen door wide open and leaps down his front steps in one bound.

                    ALEX

     Sadie, man have I missed you!

Alex swoops Sadie into his embrace. His bicep muscles squeeze like a vise as he lifts her off the ground and spins her around. She can't breathe but doesn't care, and soon it doesn't matter because Alex smothers her mouth with his--

1

"Sadie!" my mother screamed up the stairs, yanking me out of my embarrassingly passionate daydream about how Alex and I would reunite after a long, hot summer apart. "If you're going to see Alex before your dentist appointment, you better go now. We have to leave in half an hour."

"I'm going now," I lied, pulling a pillow over my face and waiting while my heartbeat returned to normal. Which was a waste of time, because seven minutes later when I walked toward Alex's front door for real, my heart resumed its frantic tempo. Why did he do this to me? After ten years of being best friends and next-door neighbors, I should be used to him by now. But I'd only been his girlfriend for eight months and eleven days, or six months and seven days if you subtracted the weeks he just spent at his cousins' house in California.

A year ago, when he came back to Massachusetts from his first summer in California, everything changed. He had shot up six inches, bulked out by twenty-five pounds, his braces were gone, his zits were cured, and on top of all that, he was bronzed and bleached blonde by the West Coast sun.

What was he coming back as this time – Apollo the Sun God? What if he had changed radically, again, and I had to get used to another new Alex? I didn't know if I could handle that. Worse, what if an even hotter Alex didn't want me anymore? Maybe he met someone else in California. What if–

"Are you coming in or what?" Alex said matter-of-factly from the other side of the screen door. "You've been standing there forever."

I opened the door, stepped inside and stood there like an idiot. I reached up to scratch my nose which suddenly itched like mad, just as Alex leaned over to kiss me. His lips landed on my fingers. Patiently, he pulled my hand away and kissed me, for ten full seconds. (I couldn't help counting.) He pulled back and sighed like someone who'd just finished a great meal.

"I've been waiting a long time for that. Eight weeks to be exact."

Before I could speak, he wrapped me in a hug that melted me to my core. Reunited. Cue that lame disco song my parents loved to slow dance to, I think mainly to drive me crazy.

Later, sitting in the car on the way to the dentist, I re-played the scene in my head. Our real life reunion had been way better than anything I scripted, because of Alex's confidence, which trumped my awkwardness.

I tried to remember exactly when he got so perfect. Was it when his looks changed? When his new bod transformed him into a sports star? Or was he always this calm and in command but I never noticed because he looked all goofy and awkward? Or because he always let me take charge when we hung out, happy to sit back and let me decide which movie to watch, which scene to re-enact, or which theme to give our next little play?

All I knew was that he was going to look amazing onstage with me in this year's school play. He was always a great character actor, but now he had leading man presence. So we had to act opposite each other this year. Had to. Preferably as the leads. We were running out of time.

Senior year. Our last play, or maybe next-to-last one, if the principal let us do a spring show, too. I was ready to help steer our beloved Crudup Drama Club on the path to another great production. After all, our old director Mr. Ellison pretty much hand-picked me at the end of last school year to help out the program's new director this year.

By the time of our first CDC meeting, the second week of school, I hadn't met said director yet, because Ms. English taught English (really) for freshmen and sophomores, not for upperclassmen. But, I'd seen her in the hallway and she was young, stylish, and hopefully up on her musical theatre. Also hopefully, she was up to the task of collaborating with me and my friends, the cast of characters who'd called CDC home for four years, because we wanted another killer show for our final year.

"Good afternoon, everyone. Thanks for coming! What a great bunch of kids we have here!" Ms. English projected out from center stage, hinting at a theatrical background, which was a good start. But her enthusiasm was over the top. "We are going to have so much fun in Drama Club this year!"

"Actually, we call it CDC, not Drama Club," said Foster from the front row of wooden auditorium seats, blowing air up at the lock of black hair falling into his eye. Shellacked with hair gel, it didn't budge.

"CDC? Like the Center for Disease Control?" She made a face as if tasting something disgusting, then literally wiped it away with a swipe of her hand. "Well, it doesn't matter what we call it. It matters what we do with it. Now, for this year's show, we're going to do a modern classic – *Seussical.*" She waited for our reaction but only a few middle-schoolers showed any excitement. "It's a great show. I've always wanted to direct it. Does anyone know it?" she prodded. "Based on Dr. Seuss? *Horton Hears A Who* and other great stories?"

"Yeah, we know it, we've even thought about doing it, and it would've been great a few years ago, but we make our own musicals now," Kristina said for the group, playing with the hair scrunchy she put in and took out a hundred times a day.

"Right, we take existing stories like *Twilight* and *Wuthering Heights* and turn them into musicals. And we're damn good at it, too," enthused Lucey, ironically since she hadn't been in either show. The bane of my existence had quit *Twilight* last fall, after beating me for the lead, because she got pregnant and morning sickness took over her life. Then, she stayed out of school to have her baby and missed *Wuthering Heights* in the spring completely.

"Sadie writes the scripts," Alex added, flashing me the megawatt smile I loved.

"Well, yes, Principal Zowicki told me you made up your own shows last year, but that was because you didn't have any money to license the rights to a real show. This year's budget includes money for the Drama Club, so we can go back to producing actual musicals. Isn't that what you want?" Her eyes opened wide and I think she instantly regretted asking our opinion.

"We'd rather be creative and write our own show and songs," Kristina stated in a flat voice that suggested she was having the same sinking feeling about this year's show that I was.

"And I had the perfect idea for this year's story: *To Kill A Mockingbird*, since it's the fiftieth anniversary of the book's publication," I said. "It's a real American classic," I tacked on pathetically, since it was obviously a lost cause.

All summer, I'd been waiting to lay my *Mockingbird* idea on the cast, which I was pretty sure was perfect. Lots of adults and students knew the story, it had great characters, and writing the script would have looked awesome on my college applications. We probably wouldn't have modernized the story like we did with *Wuthering Heights* because the setting was integral to the plot. The school Halloween pageant near the end when Scout plays a ham would have made a sweet play within a play. And creating our own lyrics for the songs...we would have killed that. Coming of age themes mixed with a *Legally Blonde* courtroom-type number or two.

It would have been serious material worthy of a Yale School of Drama applicant. Instead, I was getting a musical based on a bunch of children's books. The bottom was falling out of my future.

"What is *Seussical*, anyway?" asked Lindsay, the least theatrical of all of us. "Sounds like it's for little kids."

"No, actually many adult theatre groups perform *Seussical*," Ms. English pointed out. "And we're doing the full, grown-up version, not *Seussical Jr.*, although we might have to drop one or two of the bigger scenes, depending on how many people try out." Her enthusiasm was not contagious.

"The actors dress up like jungle animals and there's a boy who thinks too much. And an elephant and a bird that fall in love," explained Foster.

"Oh yea, we get to dress up like animals. What fun," deadpanned Ben, taking off his brown-framed glasses and rubbing a smudge with his shirt to drive home his disinterest.

"Don't we get any say in this?" asked Lucey, tossing her perfect, wavy blonde hair.

Uncertainty flickered across Ms. English's pretty face, which quickly firmed up into a stern mask. "No, I'm afraid you don't. The decision has been made, and approved. One reason Mrs. Zowicki hired me was so I could up the professionalism of your group. And the librettos and score are already on their way. This year's show is *Seussical*."

The small sighs emitted by the seniors merged into one big wave of exasperation.

"Well, do we get to do a spring show?" asked Kristina, smoothing her straight brown hair unnecessarily. "Maybe we can end our high school careers with our own production in the spring?"

"Mmm, that's unlikely. Apparently, the band director was so inspired by your two shows last year that he wants to create his own thing – a talent show or something – for the spring. I'll certainly try to get us a second show, but for now, let's concentrate on this one and see if we can get it right, shall we?" said Ms. English, ending the discussion by bounding up to the stage, surprising agile in her four-inch heels and pencil skirt, her long, blonde hair swaying with the motion. I'd kill for hair like that, smooth as glass, unlike my wavy, unruly mess.

Focus, Sadie, I told myself. You're losing control of the theatre program you co-founded. You have to do something. But I knew I'd already lost control. Completely. I really missed Mr. Ellison.

"Now, who'd like to do some get-to-know-you exercises?" she asked, looking right at the middle-schoolers, having given up on us older kids. But we were not to be silenced.

"Um, get-to-know-you exercises?" asked Lindsay, smirking and rubbing a hand through his cropped blonde hair. "Dude, we kinda all know each other already."

"Too well," said my close friend Adrienne. "After twelve years with the same kids in our classes, we're practically like brothers and sisters." She crossed her arms and her big brown eyes looked away like she was afraid she'd been rude.

Ms. English's perfect lips puckered into a pout. "Oh come on, I bet you don't know everything about each other. It'll be fun. Now everyone, form a circle on the stage." She motioned up with her hands repeatedly until all twenty-four of us stood onstage. "So, what you do, is state your name and something you especially like. So I might say, my name is Ariana and I like cats. Now you – what's your name?"

"Sadie," I said, hoping she caught the suspicion in my voice.

"Okay, Sadie, so now you say what you like, and then repeat what I said, and so on." She swept her hand toward me in a grand gesture, as if bestowing an invisible spotlight upon me.

In my best bored voice, I said, "My name is Sadie and I love–"

"Theatre!" yelled Lindsay, throwing his fist in the air.

"That's not what I was going to say!" I protested.

"Yeah, right. Of course it was. If it wasn't, what were you going to say?"

I mumbled, "I was going to say drama."

Every single one of my supposed friends cracked up, even my traitor boyfriend Alex.

Jocelyn was next because, annoyingly, she'd wormed her way between me and Alex in the circle. They'd dated for a few months junior year and I was afraid she still liked him. "My name is Jocelyn and I like–"

"Shopping," said Jocelyn's best friends Lucey and Kristina at the same time. Jocelyn nodded.

"Hey, this is fun after all," Lindsay said. "Come on, Holman, you're next." Ms. English smiled uncertainly.

"My name is Alex, and I like–"

"Sports," three people yelled at the same time, while a fourth yelled "basketball".

"This isn't how it's supposed to work," interrupted Ms. English, stepping forward into the circle. "Let the person say it. And then that person repeats what the other people said."

Lindsay nodded and stepped forward.

"Okay, I got this. I'm Lindsay, and I like...you have to guess what I'm thinking, and it's not sports 'cause we already used that one with Holman."

"Girls," said Jocelyn.

"Partying," said Lucey. Lindsay shook his head at both of them.

"Sleeping," Foster offered.

"Farting," said Ben, Foster's best friend.

"Ooh, gross, Ben," said Jocelyn as if Ben had let one go, not said the word.

"Come on. You'll never guess," Lindsay beamed.

"This game is boring, just tell us," Lucey whined, twirling a blonde curl around her finger.

"Fine. I like zombies," said Lindsay with a satisfied smile. "And oh yeah, that's Alex and he likes Sadie, and that's Jocelyn who likes having lots of clothes, and that's Sadie and she likes Alex, and that's Ariana and she likes making us do lame exercises. Your turn, Kristina."

"I think that's enough," Ms. English interjected before Kristina could go. "Let's try something else with directions that are a little easier to follow," she said sarcastically. "This exercise is called Red-Blue."

"Purple!" Lindsay shouted. We all looked at him with confused faces. "What? I thought we were supposed to name the color you get when you mix the other two colors. Since we're acting like we're in elementary school. What's next - two plus two? Or red plus yellow?"

A wrenching sigh escaped Ms. English's chest. The rise and fall of her cleavage caught Lindsay's eye, I noticed.

"Lindsay, if this is too bothersome for you, you're welcome to leave. Everyone else, please split into two groups and form circles." We reluctantly obeyed. Lindsay was the only one who seemed happy about the new game, probably because he knew it would give him more things to make fun of. Our circle was all high-schoolers, and the other mostly middle-schoolers.

"You, and you, are the starters," Ms. English said, standing between the two circles and tapping Ben and Ada Fishbein on the shoulders. "Say 'red' to the person on your left, who then says 'red' to the person next to them, and so on until you get back to the starter. Then the starter says 'blue' and it goes around the circle in the other direction."

"With all due respect, Ms. English," – man, was Kristina sucking up to the new director? – "is there a point to this?" Guess not.

"I think it's to see if we're all capable of speaking the word 'red'," Ben laughed, shaking his mop of brown hair.

"The point," Ms. English said, her patience starting to fray, "is to work together as a team, and see which circle can complete the task first. You know, I think you guys need to learn some–" and she started to sing like Aretha Franklin in the song "Respect" when she spells out the word R-E-S-P-E-C-T except Ms. English sang R-E-S-P-E-C-K.

Everyone stared at her.

Ms. English cleared her throat. "That's a line from *Seussical*. You'll know it soon enough. Anyway, are we ready? Set? Go!"

The seniors, to her dismay, took our time saying 'red', and the few underclassmen in our circle started to copy us so they wouldn't look uncool. When Foster stretched out the word for five seconds, that became the new game, seeing who could take the longest to say "red". Meanwhile, the circle of younger kids was going around for the third time.

"It looks like the middle-schoolers won for both speed and attitude," the teacher said. "Rather than wait twenty minutes for the older kids to finish setting their bad example, let's move on."

CHAPTER 2: THOSE SUMMER NIGHTS

"*P*laying Sandy must have been awesome. I bet you rocked it," Alex said, drawing circles on my pant leg with his finger as we sat side by side on my living room couch, my feet tucked under my black Belgian shepherd Kato who lay on the floor in front of us. I tried to ignore Alex's touch and focus on the summer theatre camp I'd gone to.

"It was pretty great, I have to admit. That's two leads for me now – Sandy and Bella," I pointed out unnecessarily, referring to our school production of *Twilight: The Musical* from last fall.

"Bella was better, know why?" Alex cocked his head to the side.

"Why?" I replied automatically.

"Because I got to see that one." He stopped making circles and picked up my hand. "I'm sorry I missed *Grease*. Lucey must have died when you beat her for the lead." He gave a short laugh.

"I almost died when she walked into auditions. She wasn't at camp the first day, but showed up like two minutes before auditions started on the second day. She told me later she didn't even want to be there. Her parents made her, to get her out of the house."

"Not like her to pass up a show. Why do you think she wasn't into it? It's not like the kids in Dayton would have known she left school pregnant last year." Dayton was a small nearby city that dwarfed our little town, which was so puny we called it Smalltown for its lack of just about everything.

"I'm thinking she was self-conscious about the baby weight. She's kind of heavy now, at least compared to how perfect she usually looks."

He shrugged, oblivious to Lucey's five-pound weight gain. "You said you guys got friendly. Did she ever talk to you about any of it? The baby or anything? Sharing secrets and all?"

I shivered and looked away. "Um, no, no secrets. None at all. Anyway, you were right, though, when you told me a while ago that she can be okay. Sometimes." I looked back at him, unable to avoid his beautiful green eyes for long. "She was even nice to me for a while. But it didn't last long. By the end of the show, she was back to her snobby, obnoxious self."

"So she was good as – what's the character's name – Ritzo or something?"

I shook my head and grinned. "Rizzo, Alex. And she was awesome, of course. The role was practically made for Lucey. And we skipped the plot line about Rizzo's pregnancy, to keep the show family-friendly, so awkwardness avoided."

He hmphed.

"She said she wanted Rizzo anyway, because it's such a fun part and Sandy is so lame. But honestly, Alex, she choked in the audition. I actually felt bad for her. But the competition wasn't that strong so she still got a big part."

"Okay, so that's way more than we need to talk about Lucey," Alex said, shifting to face me. "Let's talk about next year. There's something I want to tell you." The guilty look on his face made me squirm. "I looked at a couple of colleges in California when I was out there. You know, just looked. It's not like I'm seriously going to be able to go to any of them."

My throat tightened. "Then why are you telling me?" He didn't answer. I inhaled, hoping the oxygen would deliver courage. "It's okay, Alex, if you want to go to school in California, you should go to school in California." I couldn't believe how calm my voice sounded, like it was coming from someone else.

"You wouldn't even care?" He sounded crushed, not happy, so I knew I'd played that one wrong. But really, why did he bring it up if he wasn't hoping to go out west? I knew I was going to lose him at some point. It was just a matter of when.

"You gotta do what you gotta do. I mean, you know I can't let anything stand in the way of my dream to go to Yale School of Drama for grad school."

He still looked crushed but I didn't know the right thing to say.

Alex sighed and stood up. "Well, it's not like I'm going to have much choice where I go anyway. My mom can't afford anything, so I'm going wherever it's cheapest."

"Or maybe you'll get an athletic scholarship somewhere good," I encouraged.

"Yeah, maybe– Hey, why are there cop cars in my driveway?" Alex walked to the window and pushed the maroon curtain to the side. I stood up and joined him.

"Oh my God, they've got your mother!" I said, but Alex was already out the front door, Kato on his heels.

CHAPTER 3: NEW ROLES

$\mathcal{M}$rs. Holman's face usually looked older than her forty-something years, but as she shuffled to the police cruiser between two officers, she looked like a terrified kid.

"Mom, what's going on?" Alex yelled, crossing my front yard and reaching her in a few strides.

"Easy, son," said the taller of the two policemen, putting out his arm to prevent Alex from reaching Mrs. Holman. Kato slunk his head down and growled at the policeman. I grabbed the dog's collar and pulled him back a few feet.

"Officer Kelly, right?" Alex sounded amazingly calm on the surface. Only someone who knew him like I did could hear the edge of panic in his voice. "What's going on? Where are you taking her?"

"Police business, you'll be informed in good time." Officer Kelly couldn't look Alex in the eye. Or Mrs. Holman for that matter. He kept staring at the ground ten feet in front of him.

"Mom, what's happening?" Alex asked.

"Alex, honey, don't worry. There's been some kind of misunderstanding. It will all be fine." Her shoulders hunched as she coughed twice, her gray-streaked brown hair falling over her face. She brushed back the hair and stooped to get into the cruiser. I didn't see Mrs. Holman much because she worked two jobs, so I was shocked to see how frail she looked compared to the last time I saw her.

"Mom! What's the misunderstanding? Tell me!"

Mrs. Holman stopped moving and said softly to her son, as if embarrassed, "They say I stole prescription drugs from the hospital pharmacy. I'm sorry, Alex, I'm so sorry. Don't think badly of me."

"Mom, don't be ridiculous. I know you wouldn't do that. Who would say you did? Why?"

"I don't know, honey. But I have to go to the police station and answer some questions. Don't worry." She stooped down and got into the car

"Don't worry? Mom, I'm freaking out!" Outright frustration replaced the underlying panic in his voice.

"Don't worry," Mrs. Holman said again, unconvincingly, before Officer Kelly shut the cruiser door.

As the other officer started the engine and drove off, she peered at us through the tinted window looking for all the world like we were paparazzi stalking her. If it weren't so serious, the situation would have been funny.

When the cruiser was out of sight, Alex turned to me, looking more lost than I'd ever seen him. His front door slammed, making him jump and Kato growl again. Police Chief Wyatt and an officer came out, peeling off latex gloves and eyeing my dog suspiciously.

"That was a waste of time," the chief said.

"It's not like she was going to leave the drugs lying around," the young officer said. "They've probably already been sold."

From the corner of my eye, I saw Alex stiffen and lean forward. For a second, I thought he might go after the cop.

"You searched my house? You went through our stuff?" Alex's voice rose.

"Relax, son, we have a warrant," the officer mumbled, walking around Alex.

"Alex," said Chief Wyatt, "it's just standard procedure." He walked to his cruiser and opened the door. "Don't worry too much, I'm sure it will all be fine," he said, and ducked into his car.

We watched them drive off. Alex must have felt even more helpless than I did.

"Come on," I said finally, letting go of Kato and taking Alex's hand.

"Where are we going? What do we do?" he asked.

"We're going to talk to my dad, and then I have a feeling he's going to call a lawyer."

$\mathcal{A}$lex wasn't very focused when I dragged him to the next CDC meeting. Of course, I completely understood. His mother, who was a cleaning lady at the Dayton hospital, was, legit, being accused of stealing drugs – oxycodone pills, to be exact. The police said an eyewitness, another night-shift worker, saw her go into the hospital pharmacy. She was released on bail, but the hospital suspended her without pay, which wasn't helping the Holmans' stress levels. At least Mrs. Holman was able to keep working her other job, as a hostess at a local restaurant, although Alex said she was so worried about the accusation she could barely drag herself out of bed in the morning.

My parents got their lawyer on the case, at our cost because there was no way Mrs. Holman could afford it. My dad taught history at Crudup High and my mom was a partner in a big PR firm, so while we weren't rolling in it, we were a lot better off than Mrs. Holman. I would have quit school and worked three jobs if I had to, to help Alex. I couldn't stand how miserable he looked since Mrs. Holman was arrested.

Since all we could do was wait to see how the whole thing played out, I thought the make-believe world of theatre was the perfect distraction to get Alex's mind off the situation.

Fifteen minutes into the CDC meeting, make-believe seemed like an understatement. Surreal was more like it, as I watched the drama program I helped build with Mr. Ellison the past few years get hijacked by Ms. English. She was completely changing the way we did everything.

"This is a big show," she said to start the meeting. "Extravagant sets, costumes, and even the props are extensive. Then there's sound, lighting and overall stage management."

"Adrienne runs stage crew, and most of that other stuff, too," Foster interjected.

"And she's awesome at it," I felt compelled to add.

"Except costumes. Foster's better at that than I am," Adrienne said.

"That's wonderful," Ms. English said, interrupting our love-fest, "but that won't be enough. We need a lot of people to pull off this big a production and bring my vision to life. Now, I understand there aren't many kids involved in drama except those of you who are already here. And we'll need all of you in the cast. I'm counting on you to help with set painting et cetera, but we need reinforcements. That's why I'm sending this note home with you asking for your parents to help out." She handed out sheets as we made faces at each other.

"But–" started Kristina.

"We don't want–" said Sam Carter at the same time.

Both were cut off instantly by Ms. English, who obviously was ready for protest this time. "I know, I know, you guys are used to being in charge. But you can't do it all yourself. Won't it feel good to have more support, so you can focus on the acting and singing?"

"Some of us like to focus on the other stuff. She doesn't get it," Adrienne leaned over and whispered to me, her shoulder-length brown hair swinging into her face.

"Our first two parents are already on board, and you know them from last year," Ms. English continued her dictatorial soliloquy. "While I have a considerable dance and vocal background – I actually minored in theatre and have been active in performing arts all my life – I can't do the dance and music all by myself, so Denise Kent will be helping out with choreography again this year, and School Committee member Judy Fishbein has agreed to return as Music Director."

It was weird that the new music teacher wasn't involved in the school play, but we'd already figured out that Fishbein was filling the music role again, since she and Mrs. Kent were sitting right there in the auditorium with us. Kristina's mother was okay, other than a tendency to bow to Mrs. Fishbein's every demand and a thinly veiled homophobic tendency. Her choreography was decent and she was an okay instructor.

Fish-bean, on the other hand, as we called her (the correct pronunciation was fish·bine), was a total pain. She hardly let us do anything for ourselves last year. She practically took over directing from Mr. Ellison, and seriously cut into my input as assistant director. Plus, she didn't even attempt to hide her favoritism toward her daughter Ada, who was a freshman now.

So Fishbein wasn't exactly welcomed, but at least she was the devil we knew.

What about English? On one hand, she was an official triple threat – singer, dancer and actor, which was way more relevant experience than Mr. Ellison had. This was good. On the other hand, she clearly had her own vision for the show and wasn't going to let us have much say. We were merely marionettes to her puppeteer. Plus, she had this annoying habit of spelling out R-E-S-P-E-C-K during conversations, which was making us hate that part of the show before we even rehearsed it. On the other hand, as Tevye would say, maybe she could inject our program with a dose of professionalism we'd never had before. That could be helpful to the cause of getting into Yale School of Drama. On the other hand, I wasn't going to get any playwright or directing experience with *Seussical*, only acting. On the other hand–

"Auditions are next Monday and Tuesday," English was saying, "and preparation is everything. The more prepared you are, the greater your chances of landing a good role."

Kristina was nodding. The over-achiever, she was always more prepared than anyone else, whether it was an audition, a test, or college applications. Most of us, including me, hadn't even decided where to apply for college. I mean, over the summer I made a list of thirty schools with good theatre and musical theatre programs, but I was having a hard time deciding which ones to apply to. Kristina, on the other hand, already had a list of Ivy League and other A-list schools picked out, and applications started. She wrote her essay the spring of junior year. Soon, she would pick a favorite, apply early admission, and be accepted for sure.

Jocelyn was nodding because Kristina was, but her idea of audition prep probably meant picking out a new outfit and getting a manicure so she'd look her best.

In between Kristina and Jocelyn, Lucey picked at her nails and looked bored, every bit the diva who probably thought she was owed a great part since she was forced to give up the lead in her last show due to that pesky pregnancy being thrust upon her.

"Ms. English, does it matter if you've been a lead before?" asked Ben, who had had great supporting roles before but was still itching for a lead.

"What do you mean?" Ms. English said.

"Well, I mean do you want to spread the leads around, us being just a high school program and all? To be fair? Or could someone who's had a big lead before get the lead again this year?" He looked everywhere except at Foster, who was the lead in the last show.

"Hm. Interesting question." She pulled her long hair back as if she were going to put it in a ponytail, then let it drop. "How many of you have had the lead before?"

Everyone glanced around the room, not sure how to respond. Was this a trick question? Did we decrease our chances of a lead this year if we'd had a lead before?

"Be honest, now, I'm not saying it matters one way or the other."

"Jocelyn was the lead in *High School Musical*, and I was the lead in *Wuthering Heights* last year," Kristina confessed. Jocelyn nodded, completely fine with her friend speaking for her.

Lindsay's blue eyes gleamed. "Lucey won the lead of Bella in *Twilight*, but didn't actually make it onstage." He fake smiled at Lucey.

"Really? Why not?" Ms. English asked.

"I got sick and had to leave school," Lucey said, glaring at Lindsay. "Lindsay's had two leads – Tevye in *Fiddler on the Roof*, and Troy in *High School Musical*. So he's had more than anyone." She actually stuck her tongue out at him, making him shrug and laugh.

"Anyone else?" Ms. English asked, her eyes skimming the musty auditorium.

Foster and I looked at each other and nodded. "I was the male lead last year," Foster admitted, subconsciously emphasizing the word 'male' I thought. No wonder. He'd been subjected to homophobic bullying after being announced as the lead, even though he did an amazing job as the stormy, macho Heathcliff in *Wuthering Heights*.

"And I was Bella in *Twilight*. But I barely got to enjoy it 'cause I only got the lead on, legit, the day of the show, so I don't think that should count–"

"Then my getting Bella in the first place shouldn't count either," Lucey demanded.

"Geez, maybe neither one of you should count for anything," Lindsay said.

"Whoa, slow down. A little competitive, are we?" sighed Ms. English. "That's okay, it wouldn't be a drama club without some healthy competition. Anyway, I don't really care what roles you've had before." My tense shoulders relaxed for the first time all afternoon. "You're all new to me, a clean slate. However, and this may be a little different for you, I do want to know what your aspirations are. So on your audition card, I want you to write down which role you want the most." No one said anything. "Okay?"

"Wait– are you saying we can only audition for one part?" Foster asked, his dark eyes scrunching up.

"Then what if we don't get the part we try out for?" said Sam, for Foster's benefit, I think. Sam did CDC because he liked being part of the group. He didn't seem to care what kind of part he got. For Foster, though, good roles were life and death.

"Yeah, let's say you're the best choice for a big part, but you didn't ask for that part, and the second best choice did ask for the part. Does that person get the role?" I asked, trying to get my head around how this idea changed the dynamic of auditions.

"Don't overthink it, people. I just want to know what role you're most interested in. It gives me an idea what type of role you like to play. But casting is an art, not a science. In the end, I'll cast the way I think is best for the show."

"So, do looks matter?" asked Emily, who hardly ever spoke up. "Because sometimes before, someone was cast as a lead because she looked the part." She kept her eyes down rather than look at Jocelyn, who we all knew landed the role of Gabriella because of her long, dark hair, not because she was the best singer. I tried not to hold that against my former mentor, Mr. Ellison. It had been his first time casting a show, after all.

"Wow–" said Ms. English, "you guys have a lot of questions. Not used to having someone else in charge, are you? Listen, don't worry, I promise to be fair and balanced in my judging. And you can talk to me after if you have any questions about why you got the role you got. Deal?"

We nodded. What choice did we have?

I'd never felt so powerless in my entire life.

After the first meeting, when Ms. English had informed us how she was running the program this year, a bunch of us considered quitting. We were pissed off that Zowicki and English hadn't given us any say in this year's show, and that we were doing a kid show on top of that. But in the end, we weren't ready to give up our only theatrical outlet. It wasn't like Crudup High had a scriptwriting or screenwriting class to funnel our energies into. We didn't even have a drama class. So we were stuck with *Seussical*, like it or not. At least we'd have fun hanging with each other. As for the new director, the jury was still out.

CHAPTER 4: HIGH ROAD

"*I* don't know if I'm going to audition. I mean, I don't know if I should even do the show this year," Alex said, sending me spiraling into a horrible flashback to last fall when he announced he was skipping CDC in order to focus on sports. Thankfully, he came back for last year's spring show.

In some weird way, Alex was my muse. I was almost as addicted to him as I was to theatre. When he wasn't in a show with me, I felt like I was constantly missing a prop or forgetting an important line.

Still, I had to be more patient with him this year, his mother being accused of a crime and all.

"Don't you think it might help keep your mind off things to do the show?"

He sighed. "Well, CDC is a good distraction, and I want to be with you. But I need to take control of my life. Of my future. I need to get a really good job someday so I don't have to slave away at bad-paying jobs like my mom. And I need to make enough to support her, not just my own wife and kids."

"Wow, you are seriously planning ahead," I said, nudging his shoulder with mine, trying to joke around. We were sitting on the old gray picnic table in his back yard, soaking up what was probably the last of the September sun.

He refused to lighten up. He had his serious face on, which made him look ten years older. "You don't get it, Sadie. Your life is pretty well laid out for you. A theatre degree at some really good college, then Yale Drama, and no real worries about how to pay for it all. I don't have a plan, but I need one more than you. I'm the only one my mom has. And I need to be there for her.

But no one is letting me now. I'm so sick of being pushed around by cops and teachers and every other adult in the world."

Anger, sadness and frustration took turns occupying his face while he spoke. I knew the past week had been tough for him, but maybe I hadn't realized how tough.

"It's really important that I get good grades this year, and that I do awesome in soccer and basketball, because a scholarship is the only thing that's going to get me into college so I can get a decent job some day."

What could I say to that? For the first time in my life with Alex, I kept my mouth shut. He was probably right. We'd known for years that Mrs. Holman couldn't afford college. Even the state university was out of reach if they had to pay full tuition. I'd always assumed they'd find a way to get him to college, but when it came right down to it, I had no idea how. With graduation months away, this dilemma felt horribly real.

"Would you be mad? If I didn't do the show?" He kept his voice neutral so I couldn't tell what answer he wanted. I resisted the urge to say of course I wanted him to do the show. Noble guy that he was, he might actually put me before himself and his mother. I couldn't have that on my conscience. This was too serious. Too important to him. Time to take the high road. To my surprise, I didn't have to fake conviction in my words.

I took his hand. "Alex, you should do whatever is best for you and your mom. I'll be fine."

"I haven't decided for sure, you know. I'm just thinking about it and I needed to know how you'd feel." But his face relaxed an iota for the first time in a week, and I knew the decision was made.

I forced a smile but my insides were dying. There went what was probably our last chance to act opposite each other. Alex and I had made up so many shows at home, and we were an awesome team, but we would never be the leads in front of an audience larger than a few relatives and my dog Kato.

But even deeper inside, behind the part that was dying at the thought of an Alex-less show, another part of me knew he was doing the right thing. That conviction became even stronger a week later, when Mrs. Holman was taken away in an ambulance.

CHAPTER 5: DEADLY DISEASE

We'd been riding the bus home on Friday – one of the few times Alex actually rode the afternoon bus. He didn't have afternoon soccer practice because they had a game at eight that night. Usually, I was left to suffer through the painful bus ride home on my own. I could have ridden with my dad but he usually stayed after school to correct papers and I didn't want to wait for him.

The ride was painful because we were practically the only seniors on our bus. Even though we both had our junior driver's licenses, we didn't have cars to drive to school, or friends nearby with cars, so we were forced to bounce along with the middle-schoolers and underclassmen. At least they respected our position and left the back row open for us. Once, we got on the bus to find a freshman pouting in our seat. A glare from Alex sent the kid running for the middle of the bus, making us crack up because the thought of Alex actually scaring someone was so hysterical.

We usually tuned out the obnoxious shouting of the younger kids with our iPods.That day, we were sharing earbuds and staring into our laps, Alex probably thinking about his mother's arrest, me wondering what Alex was thinking, when we pulled up to our houses. I didn't notice the flashing red lights until we stood up to head for the bus door.

"What the—" Alex said, bombing down the bus aisle and leaping down the three bus steps in one jump, before running to the ambulance in his driveway.

I tried to keep up with him while fumbling with my iPod, hoodie and backpack. He glanced in the back of the ambulance and sprinted to his front door before I even hit the driveway.

Seconds later, he came back out, followed by his mother on a stretcher wheeled by two EMTs. She was conscious, thank God, and talking to Alex. He looked mad for some reason.

"This is becoming a habit for me, isn't it? Being taken away by the authorities?" She smiled but her voice sounded weak. Her pale hand clutched a small bloody towel. Alex tried to hold her other hand and walk beside the gurney but it was moving fast. He had to jog to keep up and kept losing his grip on her.

"But, Mom, what's wrong? Tell me what's wrong with her!" he yelled at one of the EMTs. In his frustration, Alex sounded like he was five. Why wouldn't anyone tell him anything? This was his mother, after all.

"Alex, I just coughed up some blood. I really don't think it's a big deal, but when I called the doctor he insisted on the ambulance. It's overkill, and I'm sorry if it scared you."

"She's coughing up blood? What does that mean?" Alex demanded of the EMTs as they fed the stretcher into the back of the ambulance. While one EMT tightened the belts around Mrs. Holman, the other turned to Alex.

"We don't know what's wrong yet. A lot of things can cause blood in the sputum. But your mother's right – it may not be a big deal at all. Try to stay calm and I'm sure she'll call you from the hospital as soon as she knows anything." The EMT's soothing voice had no calming effect at all.

"Call me? Why can't I go with you?" Alex begged.

"How old are you?"

Alex's eyes flickered and I knew he was considering lying, but he probably didn't know the right answer. I didn't either. "Seventeen." He told the truth.

"Sorry, you aren't allowed in the ambulance. Company policy," the EMT made a sad face, resumed his professional mask and climbed into the front of the ambulance.

Alex watched numbly as the ambulance drove away.

He shook his head, as if waking up. "I can take Mom's car, come on." He grabbed my arm but I stood firm.

"No, wait, there's my dad," I said, towing Alex toward my driveway instead, where my father's car was pulling in. "He'll take us to the hospital."

$\mathcal{A}$fter two torturous days filled with multiple trips to see Mrs. Holman in the hospital, lots of waiting, and way too little information, Alex and I were hanging around in my back yard, killing time until Dad got home to take us to see Mrs. Holman again. Alex aimlessly dribbled a basketball while I tightrope-walked along the cracks in the walkway that threaded around the patio area. Kato lay on the back steps, trying to doze but starting awake every time the basketball bounced near him. Through the open kitchen window, I heard Dad say hello to Mom, so I grabbed the ball from Alex and started toward the back door.

"John, I've been waiting for you," we heard my mother say. "I have an update on Jenny and it's not good."

```
(SADIE and ALEX freeze at the door.
SADIE puts her forefinger to her lips
and motions ALEX to a spot under the
kitchen window where they crouch and
listen.)

          MR. PERKINS

You saw her today? How is she feeling?

          MRS. PERKINS

Well, she says she feels okay. But she
looks horrible. Very weak and pale. But
listen, they think they figured out
what's wrong with her. They want to run
more tests to be sure, but they think
they know, finally.

          MR. PERKINS

Wendy-- What is it?

          MRS. PERKINS

(Sighs audibly. SADIE takes ALEX's hand
and squeezes.)
```

She has TB. It's called "Active TB" as opposed to "Latent TB".

MR. PERKINS

You mean tuberculosis? Seriously? I thought that disease was pretty much wiped out.

MRS. PERKINS

Nope. I looked it up while I was waiting for you. Thirteen-thousand new cases a year in this country.

MR. PERKINS

Dear God. Is it-- What's the prognosis?

(ALEX squeezes SADIE's hand so hard it hurts.)

MRS. PERKINS

It's curable, but the treatment is extensive. She has to stay in the hospital for a few weeks, and then she can probably come home but will need medicine for months.

(ALEX's grasp on SADIE's hand loosens.)

And, the X-ray showed scarring on her lungs. That might even mean surgery at some point.

MR. PERKINS

Well, overall, that's still a relief. At least it's not deadly. And it's not something like cancer.

Okay, let's get the kids over to the hospital to see her. Are you going to tell Alex what she has, or let her do it?

                    MRS. PERKINS

John, wait. We have to talk about Alex. Jenny said the Department of Child Services has already been there, talking to her about Alex.
They might not let him stay at home as long as Jenny's in the hospital.

                    MR. PERKINS

What? But it's only for a few weeks.

                    MRS. PERKINS

It <u>might</u> be a few weeks. But even if it is, they don't want to let him stay alone because he's not eighteen yet. I guess it might be possible with a waiver from the court or something, but that would take weeks or even months to get. And there's the whole stealing thing. They're acting like she's not a fit mother. So they're talking about a foster home, or him going to stay with relatives. But his only relative is that aunt in California.

                    MR. PERKINS

That's ridiculous. Let's just pile more upheaval on that family. (Pause) Hey, why doesn't he stay with us? He practically lives here anyway.

                    MRS. PERKINS

Well, that's what concerns me. I'd love to help, and you know Alex is like family, but he and Sadie are so close, and I don't want them getting closer. If you know what I mean.

(ALEX and SADIE stop breathing.)

MR. PERKINS

Hmm. That could be too close for comfort.

MRS. PERKINS

Too close for my comfort, anyway. You know about the situation in my family, and how hard that was. We can't risk anything like that happening.

MR. PERKINS

And I guess we couldn't watch them every second. Even if I came home right after school, it would be easy for them to find ways and times to be alone. Which they can kind of do anyway, you realize, but why make it easier for them? He is a teenage boy, after all.

(SADIE looks nervously at ALEX, but he is glaring into space.)

Who knows? Maybe he has TB too, and he'll end up in the hospital with his mother.

MRS. PERKINS

John, that's not even funny. But speaking of who else might have it, we all have to be tested, since we've been in contact with Jenny. They're testing everyone at the hospital too.

Anyway, let's get the kids and get over to the hospital. Maybe there'll be an update on the Alex situation. I just have to grab my purse.

(Outside the kitchen window, SADIE starts to rise. ALEX holds her back.)

ALEX

Sadie, I can't go to California. And I can't go to a foster home. How will I get to see my mother that way? I need to keep an eye on her.

SADIE

I know. And it's senior year. You have to be here for senior year.

(They stand, facing each other, heads down, thinking. After a minute, they look at each other.)

ALEX

You know what we have to do.

SADIE

(Nods.) I think so.

(MR. PERKINS' keys jingle as he approaches the back door, making Kato jump up, tail wagging.)

Let's talk later, when we're alone.

(SADIE and ALEX enter the house.)

CHAPTER 6: BOMBSHELL

"*A*re you putting down Mayzie?" Alex said into my ear, making me jump ten feet.

"Alex! God, you scared me. What are you doing here?" I said, erasing the scribble I'd made on my audition card when he startled me.

"I decided to try out after all," he said, making me grin uncontrollably. "I figured why make myself even more miserable than I already am by missing the chance to hang with you? But I'm putting myself down for ensemble, okay? I can't commit the time for a lead, if I even got one."

I nodded and hugged him quickly and ferociously. Alex in a bit part was better than no Alex at all. I handed him a blank audition card and pencil from the piles on the table in the music room.

"So, you put Mayzie, right?" he asked again.

I'd lost sleep over which role to try out for, like most of the kids trying out. Mayzie and Gertrude were the biggest female roles, and I definitely wanted one, but I went back and forth a hundred times on which one. Gertrude was a nerdy, insecure bird with some adorable solos. Mayzie was a colorful, pill-popping, irresponsible bird who gives away her own egg. She had some gutsier, brasher solos.

After playing Sandy in *Grease* over the summer, I kind of wanted to switch things up and play Mayzie. But I had to consider the competition, too. I wasn't too worried about Jocelyn, who was trying out for Gertrude, since she peaked freshman year. Kristina and Lucey were bigger concerns. Kristina decided early on she was auditioning for Gertrude too, so she was out of the way if I went for Mayzie.

For ages, Lucey wouldn't tell anyone what she wanted to do, so I had to be coy too, because I was afraid she would choose whatever role I did, just to spite me. Even though we'd been sort of friends during summer theatre camp, she was probably the most competitive of all of us, and I knew she was pissed when I beat her for Sandy. She was probably dying to get revenge on me, get the role I wanted, and re-gain her role as queen of CDC.

And she probably would win. She'd beat me fair and square for Bella in *Twilight*. I only got that role when she left school. I so did not want to go up against Lucey again, especially a Lucey looking for vengeance. I would rather compete against Kristina and hope that she wouldn't get the lead twice in a row. Plus, Kristina was more like me – a strong, clear singer who sometimes sounded fantastic, but neither of us had the ability to belt like Lucey did.

So, I waited for Lucey's decision, and worked twice as hard, preparing for Gertrude *and* Mayzie. Not even Alex could wrangle an answer out of Lucey. Finally, a few days before auditions, she announced she was trying out for Gertrude. The rumor was she wanted a clean-cut role to repair her reputation. I didn't care about her motivation, just her decision. So, based on her decision, my decision was made. I would audition for Mayzie.

"Let me see," Alex said grabbing my audition card, impatient of waiting for my answer. "Oh good, yeah, Mayzie. When do you go in?"

"I'm after Foster, who's in there now, trying out for Horton."

"Okay, I'm going to leave you alone to center or whatever it is you do. I'll go fill out my card." He kissed my cheek. "Break a leg, Sade."

He turned away but didn't get far because he stopped to stare at Kristina rushing up to us, her doe eyes wide.

"Sadie, ohmygod I have to tell you something!" She grabbed my arm. "Lucey lied. She's going out for Mayzie." Kristina pulled a long stray strand of hair out of her mouth. "She was afraid of pissing you off, Alex, so she kept it a secret until now, even from me, I swear."

A twenty pound bag of bricks landed on my chest. "Great. Unbelievable. Is it her mission in life to make me miserable?"

"And here she comes," Alex said, frowning. Kristina quickly turned and strolled casually away.

Lucey's flowery perfume reached me ten seconds before she did. I watched her sway up to us, her confidence, as always, flooding me with jealousy among other unhelpful feelings.

"Look at you two, so cute," she said sweetly. "I can't believe you're still together, after everything that happened at theatre camp this summer. You know, that guy you were kissing and all." She looked innocently from me to Alex and back again. "Oh, wait– did I say something I shouldn't have? My bad. Anyway, good luck in auditions, Sadie," she said, emphasizing the taboo words *good luck*.

I felt like all the air had been sucked out of the room. My chest hurt. My head spun. Lucey, Mayzie, Gertrude, Alex, summer camp. Shit, focus, Sadie. The audition. Mine was in seconds. Should I switch and audition for Gertrude? I walked mechanically toward the auditorium to get away from the competing voices in my head, and to avoid looking Alex in the eye.

"Sadie," Alex said slowly from behind me. "What did she mean about summer camp? What happened there?" He grabbed my arm. I said nothing. "Are you going to tell me or do I have to ask Lucey?"

I bit my lip. I'd tried scripting this moment in my head a bunch of times, but I kept falling back on the hope that we'd never have to have this discussion.

"It was nothing, Alex, nothing. Really. Can we talk about it later, please? It was nothing, and it didn't mean anything."

"I think you doth protest too much," he said, looking like he'd been crushed by the same twenty-pound bag of bricks previously found on my chest. "Maybe you can tell me the truth later. I hope so," he said, and walked away.

"Aaaaargh," I said, clenching my fists, tears immediately filling my eyes.

The auditorium door opened. "Sadie, what is wrong with you? This is no way to prepare for your moment in the spotlight," Foster said, closing the door behind him. "Jesus, you look like you've seen a ghost. What's wrong?"

He pulled me into a hug as tears flowed like hot lava down my cheeks.

"Lucey– Lucey told Alex I kissed another guy over the summer, and now Alex is mad at me, and I never meant to hurt him, and I hate Lucey, and she's going out for Mayzie, she tricked me and I hate her–"

"You said that part already. But that's okay, some things bear repeating." He patted my shoulder like he was trying to burp a baby. "Slow down and tell me. *Did* something happen over the summer?"

The auditorium door opened again and Ms. English poked her blonde head out. "Sadie Perkins, you're next," she said cheerily.

"She'll be right there," Foster said, shielding me and my tears from the director with his tall frame. Ms. English disappeared. "Listen, you can tell me your transgressions later. What matters now is going in there and kicking ass and getting that part so that witch doesn't get it. Mayzie is *yours*. Do you hear me?" I nodded into his shoulder.

Foster pushed me back from his chest and looked in my eyes. "Sadie, remember during *Wuthering Heights* when I was freaking out about the text bully and you gave me advice to use onstage? Do you remember what you said?"

I did but I was too upset to talk, so I shook my head.

"You said to channel it. I used that negative energy for Heathcliff and it worked. So it's your turn. Channel your frustration and anger at Lucey into this audition. Mayzie isn't a loose, bad bird for no reason. Life was bad to her. She's fighting for survival. And so are you. So go in there and be strong. Fight on that stage as if your life depended on it."

I wiped at my tears with my forefinger, careful not to smudge my mascara any more than it probably already was.

"Are you ready? Are you okay?" Foster smoothed my hair repeatedly until I nodded.

"Good. Now, break. A. Leg." He shoved me toward the auditorium door. "And we'll break Lucey's neck later," he added for moral support as I inhaled deeply, three times, and pulled open the door.

CHAPTER 7: MAKING UP IS HARD TO DO

𝒻or the first time in my entire life, I wasn't obsessed with re-playing my audition over and over in my head during the days we waited for the cast list to come out. Guess I could thank Lucey for giving me something else to worry about.

After the auditions, Alex went to soccer practice so I didn't see him again until dinner. Mom insisted he eat with us, as she had every night since Mrs. Holman went into the hospital. I didn't even taste the food I picked at as Alex and I avoided looking at each other. I did notice my parents trading glances a few times, which reminded me of the plan Alex and I concocted the other day after overhearing their conversation. But none of that seemed to matter now.

My mother didn't even make us help with the dishes after dinner, probably because it was pretty clear Alex and I were having a fight. He told my mother he was going home to start his homework. He looked at me and then toward the door with a grim face. I followed, feeling like I was going onstage in the world's worst drama.

We leadenly walked to his house and sat on his porch. I shivered, wishing I'd grabbed a jacket.

Alex heaved a sigh. "Are you going to say anything? Anything at all?"

"What do you want me to say?" I asked. Lame.

"I want you to tell me what happened at theatre camp. What was Lucey talking about?" Without looking at him, I felt his eyes drilling into me.

Tears leaked out of my eyes before I even started talking.

                    SADIE

(Looking at her hands in her lap.)

I missed you so much this summer, Alex.

                    ALEX

I missed you, too. Keep going.

                    SADIE

So there was this guy at camp, named
Luke, who was kind of after me. I know,
weird.

                    ALEX

It's not weird at all. Keep going.

                    SADIE

He goes to Yale School of Drama and he
was one of the camp counselors. He was
like twenty-three I think.

So he kept flirting with me, and asking
me out and stuff, and I kept saying no,
I had a boyfriend. Then one day, he
says, "Hey, have you seen what your
boyfriend's up to in California?" I
didn't know what he was talking about,
but he and Lucey were pretty friendly so
I'm guessing she told him about you.

So he pulls up Facebook on his phone and
goes to Scott Miller's page to show me a
picture--

                    ALEX

Scott Miller? My cousin?!

SADIE

I know, strange, right? Luke and Scott were friends at UCLA.

So he shows me this picture of you kissing a pretty blonde girl on the cheek, and while I was wondering why I didn't see that photo on your Facebook page, he kissed me.

(Continues looking in her lap.)

ALEX

Then what happened?

SADIE

Nothing, I swear. I still refused to go out with him and he finally gave up. We only kissed the one time, really Alex.

ALEX

"We only kissed"? "We only kissed"? So you kissed him back?

(SADIE's eyes and mouth open wide in horror.)

You know, my life's pretty shitty right now, with my mom in the hospital and accused of a crime and college more important than ever but I have no idea how I'm going to get there or where I'm going to go. I thought I could count on you at least.

SADIE

(Shocked and hurt that he didn't forgive her immediately.)

Well, what about you? You kissed that
girl. I should be mad, too.

ALEX

That was nothing, as I'll explain in a
second. But I want to know why you look
so guilty. And why didn't you tell me
all this in the first place instead of
making me drag it out of you? You're
making it seem like a big deal.

SADIE

(Anger giving her strength, she stands
up to her full five-foot-five-inch
height.)

Alex, you're the one making a big deal
of it. It was nothing.

(Stomps back to her house.)

Not even the words "Assistant Director Sadie Perkins" in the *Wuthering Heights* program pulled me out of my Alex funk. The next day, he had driven his mother's car to school so we didn't see each other on the morning bus, for the first time ever. And he'd ignored me, blatantly, all day in classes and during lunch.

So there I was on Tuesday at five thirty, absent-mindedly flipping through my collection of programs from all the shows I'd been in and shows I'd seen. I loved to spread them out on my bed, organizing them by color, and then by year, and then alphabetically by show. Or sometimes I'd put them in order by favorite role, or smallest bit part to largest role.

None of that helped my mood, though, so I was sitting there fanning my face with the *Fiddler on the Roof* program from sophomore year when Mom showed up in the bedroom doorway.

"Why didn't you go to the hospital with me and Alex to see his mom?" she asked, leaning against my spotlight-yellow door jamb, her shoulder-length auburn hair pulled back in a stubby ponytail.

"Um, just too much homework," I muttered, scooping up my programs.

"And I can see how much homework you're getting done," she said, the blue eyes I wished I had inherited squinting with sarcasm. "Listen, we need to talk. How are things with Alex these days?" she said. I didn't know what answer she was looking for and didn't care. But in the back of my head, behind the part that was extremely mad at Alex for being extremely mad at me, was a vague reminder of the plan Alex and I dreamed up a few days ago. It was easy to play my part.

"Eh. I think maybe he's going to hook up with Lucey since they both love to make my life miserable," I said, maybe with more venom than the situation called for. Inside, I felt like a traitor for even speaking badly about Alex.

"You mean you broke up?" she asked, sounding hopeful.

"That would be putting it mildly. I could care less if I ever see Alex Holman again."

"Oh, that's good. Because he's moving in for a while."

My mouth dropped open as I looked up at her.

"He either stays with us or goes to a foster home. We can't let him live with strangers."

"Why not?" I asked.

My mother blinked, twice. "Well, because he's like family. Social Services is insisting he stay with someone, even though he's almost eighteen, because he's going to need Directly Observed Therapy for nine months. D-O-T they call it." She watched for my reaction. I gave none. "They're going to let your father and me take responsibility for his daily medicine, so a nurse doesn't have to come here every day." I turned my attention back to my pile of programs.

"Don't you even want to know why he needs DOT?" I knew it was best to avoid her stare when she started probing like this, so I focused on fanning out my programs like a deck of cards.

"Sure. Why?" I asked, straightening my red *High School Musical* program.

"Because Alex has Latent TB. He's not contagious, but he needs almost a year of antibiotics to get rid of it." I made no reaction. I felt her annoyance building. "And in case you're wondering, none of us have it. The results of our skin tests came in. We're all okay." A strange, sad wave moved through my body but outside I was still.

She sighed heavily. "You know, Sadie, I admit I'm actually relieved that you two aren't dating now. I got the same idea from Alex in the car. But you will have to get along if you're going to co-exist under the same roof for a while."

"How long's a while?" I asked, finally looking at her, trying to cloud the concern I felt with the indifference the part called for.

"They don't know yet. Best case is a few weeks, if Jenny responds well to the antibiotics."

"When? When is he moving in?"

"We'll wait 'til this weekend when it's not so busy. He can use Jesse's room." She turned to leave but looked back from outside the doorway. "I'm taking Alex to the hospital again after soccer practice tomorrow. Do you want to come?"

I stared at my pile of programs. "I don't know. Do you think I should?" I sensed her eyes boring into the top of my head.

"Actually, you can't. They've got Jenny in a special room and they're only allowing family in. So Alex, basically. I have to talk to her on the phone from the other side of this glass divider."

I looked up. "Then why did you ask me?"

"I just wondered if you wanted to come or not." And she left.

CHAPTER 8: RESPECK

"Can you believe she didn't even post the cast list? She doesn't do *anything* the way we used to," Foster whispered to me as we sat impatiently in the auditorium, waiting for Ms. English to start the meeting. "She-is-dri-ving-me-cra-zy," he sang, mimicking the teacher's constant singing of the *Seussical* R-E-S-P-E-C-K line from the song "Biggest Blame Fool".

"I know. Making us wait until now is inhumane," I whispered back, scanning a clump of my hair for split ends. Okay, that was an overstatement, as the amount of time we had to wait to hear who got what role was the same as other years. But our normal routine of rushing up to the music room door to see the posted cast list had been disrupted.

"All right, everyone ready?" Ms. English projected from the stage edge where she sat, swinging her boot-clad legs. "Here we go. Horton the Elephant will be played by Ben Madison."

Ben let out a whoop of surprise, followed by a more cool, "Yeahhh." I was happy for him. Ben's voice was great – maybe the strongest of the guys – but his acting was wooden. Maybe that would work in the role of an insecure, downtrodden pachyderm.

"JoJo will be played by Max Bernstein." Middle-schooler. Figured.

"As the Cat in the Hat, we'll have Lindsay Houston. Yes, Lindsay, there is a place for your whimsical, sometimes biting commentary in this show. But, there is *no* place for a disrespectful attitude. I expect to see some R-E-S-P-E-C-K out of you," she said.

No one laughed except her, so she resumed her lecture of Lindsay. "Step out of line and I'll can your butt in two seconds flat. Understood?" She cocked her head at him.

"Yes, Ms. English," Lindsay drew out condescendingly, but I was pretty sure he was psyched with his role and unlikely to screw it up.

"The role of Gertrude McFuzz goes to Emily Breyer." Whoa, big upset. Jocelyn and Kristina gasped. Kristina's eyes immediately filled. Jocelyn shrugged, tossed her head and made a phft noise. Ben and Emily, who were dating, beamed at each other. That was some casting to type. Emily practically was Gertrude. She'd do a good job with it.

"Kelly White will be the Sour Kangaroo, Foster Cordeiro will be Mr. Mayor, and Kristina Kent will be Mrs. Mayor. The Bird Girls will be Lucey Landau, Aimee Sparks and Jocelyn Meyer. The Wickersham Brothers will be played by–" Ms. English droned on with the rest of the cast announcements, but my name was never mentioned. What was going on?

She'd mentioned all of the seniors by now except me. Sam got the clover-stealing eagle Vlad Vladikoff and Big Jason was General Genghus Khan Schmitz. Sam would be happy. Vlad was a small part but Sam's biggest ever. Jason would be pissed. He was always typecast as the biggest, meanest or oldest character.

But she hadn't said Mayzie. Did I get Mayzie? Did I get anything? Had I bombed that badly in the audition? I was afraid to ask, even though she'd finished reading out the names.

Adrienne was watching me. "You didn't say Mayzie. Who got Mayzie?"

"Didn't I? How could I forget, since she gave one of the best auditions? The role of Mayzie goes to Sadie Perkins."

A smile with a mind of its own took over my face. I'd done it. I'd beat out Lucey, for the first time ever. Adrienne gave me an awkward hug from her seat next to me, which I awkwardly returned.

"Go Sadie, go Sadie," Foster chanted.

Ms. English continued on, talking about the rehearsal schedule and her expectations, but the bubble of satisfaction around my head muffled her words. I couldn't wait to tell Alex. Oh wait, that wasn't happening since he was still pissed off at me. At least Foster and Adrienne were there for me.

41

As it turns out, so wasn't pretty much everyone else, giving me props afterward and really seeming to mean it. My chest swelled more with each congratulations. Lucey, of course, did not talk to me. Kristina suggested I stay away from Lucey until she cooled down.

"I think she blew her audition," Kristina confided to me and Adrienne. "I think all the games she was playing backfired on her. In the end, she wasn't even sure which role she wanted. Can you believe she's already tried to get me to switch from Mrs. Mayor to a Bird Girl, so I can be with her and Jocelyn? If she doesn't win, she doesn't want anyone else to, either." Kristina rolled her eyes as Ms. English joined our small group.

"Everyone okay here?" she asked, smiling.

"We were just congratulating Sadie," Kristina said, nobly I thought.

"Well, you all did a great job. Sadie, I'm looking forward to seeing your Mayzie brought to life. Although you might want to tone it down a little. Your audition was a little...aggressive. We do want the audience to like Mayzie, after all."

"*T*hat's the last of it," I heard my dad say to Alex as they lugged his things into Jesse's room across the hallway from my room. My parents hadn't even asked me to help. Having a massive fight with your boyfriend had its advantages.

"Thanks, Mr. Perkins," Alex said. I heard his door shut and him moving stuff around.

How was I going to stand this? This was awkward to infinity. Even if Alex and I were normal again, him living here would change my entire routine. No more walking around in the holey T-shirt I called pajamas. No more slipping into the bathroom in my bra and underwear. No more singing loudly in the shower, not caring if I went off-key. No more scratching my butt or my breast if it got itchy. I was going to have to change everything, and be on my best behavior all the time.

I was sharing a bathroom with my boyfriend. How scary was that? I had tampons and pads and everything in there. He was going to know I used clinical strength deodorant for my smelly pits, and concealer for my zits. He was going to be naked in the shower on the other side of my bedroom wall. And I was going to be naked in the shower with him in the house.

I sighed so loudly from my floor where I lay staring at the ceiling that Kato padded over and slurped me a kiss with his velvety, black-spotted tongue. When he looked down at me, his black furry forehead sagged and wrinkled, and his pointed ears tilted forward, making him look extra concerned. I sighed again and rubbed his head.

This wasn't going to work. I didn't know if I could stand having Alex this close if everything was good between us. I knew I couldn't stand having him so close with us fighting. It was torture.

And my guilt was adding to the torture. The truth was, I had kissed – no, let's be honest – I'd made out, with Luke. Only for a minute, but in that weak minute, I cheated on Alex. The Facebook photo of Alex kissing that girl had confused me, and I'd always wondered what it would feel like to kiss someone besides Alex or Nigel, the exchange student I sort of dated junior year. So I succumbed. Worst of all, I liked it. Kissing Luke was fun. For a few seconds, I forgot about Alex. I was sure that whatever happened between Alex and the girl in the picture, it wasn't as bad as what I did.

After a while, I heard him leave Jesse's room, go down the stairs and out my front door, and then I thought I heard the muffled sound of his own front door opening and closing. I spent the next few hours writing a note. An apology. A text wasn't personal enough. I wasn't going to be able to talk to him in front of my parents, as if he would even let me. I needed to put my thoughts on paper. I was better at writing than talking anyway. I threw out a bunch of handwritten drafts. I switched to the computer to think better, and ended up writing scripts of the normal talks I wished he and I were having. I made myself go back to the apology note time after time.

A few hours later, I heard him talking to my parents downstairs, coming up and going into Jesse's room. I listened to him go in the bathroom a few times, and tried to figure out what he was doing from the muffled sounds coming through the wall.

Finally, at midnight, when everyone was quiet in their bedrooms, I snuck out.

In case my parents were still awake, I changed course and went to the bathroom, shutting the door from the outside. I tiptoed to Jesse's door – Alex's door – and slid the note underneath.

From behind my almost-closed door, I saw the light appear in the crack under his bedroom door. I waited. And waited. After an eternity, I heard his door open with I swear the world's longest creak. I quickly shut my door all the way and held my breath.

"Alex, need anything?" Dad said in the hallway, making me jump. Man, who knew he could move so fast?

"Um, just using the facilities, Mr. P," Alex muttered.

"All right then, good night."

I didn't hear Dad's door shut after he padded back to his room. I did hear Alex's shut a few minutes later.

I lay down for a restless night.

The school bus never looked so good.

Over breakfast, I was pretty sure Alex was ready to talk, because of the glances he sent me. But we had to keep up the charade over the eggs and bacon Mom insisted on feeding us. Once a month or so she'd get on a kick of feeding us real breakfasts, at least for a day or two, until she had an early meeting and went back to her routine of leaving the house before Dad and I did.

"You got my note?" I asked stupidly as soon as Alex and I plopped down on the worn leather seat of the bus.

"I did." His seriousness scared me. "And you are wrong about so many things. Did you know that?"

I swallowed hard. "What do you mean?" I choked out. The morning sun wafting in the window made the stubble on his chin glint.

"Let's see," he said, pulling the note from his jeans pocket and unfolding it. "'*I know I'm not a very good girlfriend. I always say or do the wrong thing.*' That's two– no, three things wrong already." I looked at him to see if he was joking. A sliver of a smile touched his lips, reassuring me. Thank God, we were going to get through this.

"You *are* a good girlfriend, and you only say and do the wrong thing *sometimes*." I nodded while he continued. "'*But I want to be there for you.*' Nothing wrong there. I like that part. '*Can we just be friends again?*' No, we can't just be friends again, because you're way more than a friend to me. Okay?" I nodded. "And I hope I'm way more than a friend to you. Am I?" I nodded again.

"'*I'm really sorry about the kiss, and that I didn't tell you sooner. I was afraid you would leave me, or hate me, which would be worse.*'" Alex sighed and turned to me. "Sadie, I could never hate you. And I'll never leave you. You'll have to leave me. Why don't you get that?"

"Okay," I whispered.

"I love you. Don't you know that?" My heart skittered. I love you too, Alex Holman, I heard in my head, but my mouth wouldn't open. Alex glanced at the oblivious rows of kids in front of us and kissed me quickly. He didn't seem to be waiting for an answer. I loved him even more for that.

"Oh, that reminds me, there's more, right?" He looked down at the note. "'*P.S. Kissing you is way more fun. P.P.S. I mean, kissing him wasn't fun at all. P.P.P.S. It doesn't matter either way because it will never happen again.*' You know, for a writer, sometimes you really don't know when to end a scene."

He took my hand and my heart cracked open and started re-forming into a happier, healthier organ.

"You can talk now, you know," he said, his sea-green eyes peering into my mud brown ones.

I swallowed. "I know. I'm just trying to figure out how to ask you about something without sounding like a jerk."

"Go ahead," he said.

"Your kiss. You haven't explained about your kiss on Facebook." My voice trailed off, not sure if I wanted to hear the answer.

"Oh. Okay, so here's what happened. A bunch of us were at the beach and it was this girl's birthday. She wanted pictures of herself with every single guy there kissing her. It was stupid, I thought, but she's good friends with my cousin so I did it. Only on the cheek. Did you see the whole album? She posted like twenty pictures all of guys kissing her. So it was nothing."

"Oh," was all I could say.

I felt like an idiot. If I hadn't been so shocked and upset when I saw the photo, Luke wouldn't have been able to kiss me, and none of this would have happened. I should have had more faith.

Still, even with my weaknesses glaring me in the face, I felt a hundred pounds lighter.

We sat quietly for a minute.

"Alex, what are we going to do at home? Now that we're back together again. I mean, we are, right?"

Alex shook his head. "We were never not together, Sade." He squeezed my hand. "We have to pretend to still be mad at each other, though. Like we were going to do anyway, so your parents will let me stay with you. Got it?"

It was so weird to have him directing us instead of me.

"Yeah, I guess that's our only choice. But do we have to be *so* mad at each other? I don't think I can act that way for long."

He bit his lip and squinted. "We could probably tone it down a little. Co-exist kind of peacefully, you know, but not actually being friendly."

"And do you think we should plan what conversations to have in front of my parents? You know, write mini-scripts? You know I work better with a script."

He shook his head. "We have to do this as we go. Think of it as improv."

I groaned. "You know I hate improvisation."

He grinned. "I know. Because you're not in charge. But just think how much better prepared you'll be for drama school after weeks of doing this."

He looked so earnestly goofy, I had to smile back.

The bus pulled up in front of Crudup High and we put our masks back on.

CHAPTER 9: HOPE

*L*ife was stable for a few weeks after that.

Rehearsals started. I missed Alex, who hadn't tried out in the end, after Lucey dropped her stupid bombshell about summer camp, so I poured myself into developing my character. I tried a few approaches. Should Mayzie be a lovably carefree and slightly irresponsible bird, an obnoxious self-centered one, or somewhere in between? There was a lot of leeway in how to interpret her. I thought about asking Ms. English's advice but the time was never right.

I loved my solos in "Mayzie in Palm Beach", the reprise of "How Lucky You Are", and of course "Amayzing Mayzie". Actually, all the songs in this show were pretty great. And the script was clever. We even starting using phrases that sounded so silly at first, like "A person's a person no matter how small", in our everyday talk.

Still, to keep our pride intact, the seniors made one last attempt to get Ms. English to let us adapt *Seussical* into a modern version with our own songs. No go. She patiently explained that changing the show would violate copyright laws, unless it was a satire of the original, which it wouldn't be. We put our frustrations aside and slid into Seuss world.

School was school. I had way too much homework and wondered when the senior slide officially started. The girls soccer team was losing as many games as they won, but the boys team was kicking butt. The cross-country team was apparently the best ever, but since I had no idea how to even watch a cross-country race, I didn't pay much attention.

The investigation into Mrs. Holman's supposed crime continued, painfully slow. The police tried to question her a few more times but her doctor refused to let them because she was so weak. And her treatment in the hospital continued, painfully slow. Alex said they stuck her with needles every day, and made her spit into cups and have repeated chest X-rays. Her TB wasn't responding as planned, so she was stuck in the hospital indefinitely, until the doctors cleared her to go home.

Alex took his daily antibiotic under the watchful eye of my mother or father, who signed a daily statement practically in blood affirming they'd personally seen him take the medicine. No place for trust in the TB world, apparently.

A few weeks after the doctors confirmed that Mrs. Holman and Alex had TB, Principal Zowicki announced that every single student, teacher and employee at Crudup High was going to be tested.

"Where's Alex?" I asked at breakfast on TB Day, trying to sound grumpy and indifferent.

"He's sleeping in today. I'm not making him go to school," Mom said, sounding like Alex's parent. As always, I tried not to seem too interested, but luckily she kept talking, answering my unasked question. "It's going to be a tough day, with everyone at school having the TB test. I don't want him to feel awkward or uncomfortable, since he's basically the reason some of the parents insisted everyone get tested."

I hmphed. "It's a little late to worry about awkwardness. Everyone's been calling him TB Boy for ages."

"I know, but that doesn't make it right. Poor Alex feels like a pariah. So I'm letting him play hooky today." That seemed hugely unfair to me, but maybe there was an opportunity in her special treatment of him.

"What about me? I've already had the test, so I don't need to go in either." The vision of a day with Alex swirled around in a fog in the back of my brain while I reflexively touched the spot on my forearm where the nurse had pricked the skin for my TB test.

"Sadie, it's not the same and you know it. You can go to school."

She stood up, taking her empty cereal bowl with her. My cloudy vision of quality time with Alex popped like a balloon stuck with a very sharp needle.

*A*lex and I had entered this alternate universe. At home, we pretended to tolerate each other but to be broken up. At first, we thought school would be our haven, where we could be ourselves, but we quickly realized that with my father teaching at Crudup, we'd have to pretend to be broken up at school, too. We used the bus ride every morning to de-brief our performances of the past twenty-four hours and make any adjustments to our unwritten script. Unless we were tired. Then we'd just hold hands and sit quietly for fourteen minutes.

Then, because *Seussical* rehearsals apparently were going too well for Mrs. Fishbein's liking, she started taking more control. I think secretly she wanted to get Ms. English tossed and be the director herself. She started getting in the teacher's way, and interrupting rehearsals to make tons of stupid suggestions. Ms. English had to listen, because as a School Committee member, in a way Fishbein was English's boss.

As Fishbein got pushier, we got antsier and more unhappy with the tight rein the adults were holding on us. We'd given up making suggestions on anything like the blocking or the props. When I volunteered an idea for a new harmony in "How Lucky You Are" it was shot down before my mouth even closed. And anytime one of us veered from Dictator English's tight direction, she'd stop rehearsal and correct us. "It's better this way," she'd insist. I'd never worked with a director who insisted on every little thing being done her way. It took all the fun out of it. I had to focus on following her directions like it was a test or something, instead of bringing Mayzie to life my way.

"There's no room for improv in a Tony-winning musical," Fishbein spat out after my absolutely last suggestion, her dark brown bob bobbing.

"Actually, it was only nominated for a Tony," Ms. English said, but Fishbein wasn't listening.

Ms. English got tired of being ignored, and must not have cared about her job after all, because she started fighting back. The two adults bickered in front of us sometimes, about every aspect of the show. It reminded us way too much of Mr. Ellison and Mr. Lord junior year. Kristina overheard the two women arguing once about a spring show. She said Ms. English was trying to convince Fishbein to use her influence as a School Committee member to get us the money for a second show, and Fishbein said maybe a talent show was a better idea because it would present more equal opportunities for all the students regardless of their age. In other words, she wanted Ada to have a bigger piece of the spotlight.

Then, there were the parents. As if we didn't have enough adults invading our theatre, Ms. English was true to her word and enlisted a bunch of volunteers to help. During rehearsals, we were pushed and pulled by two parent costumers, and our backstage time was constantly interrupted by mothers wanting to know if we owned a spare bathtub or circus program for props. As the mothers infiltrated our production, I would have felt badly for Ms. English who had to manage them all, if it hadn't been her idea in the first place.

Rehearsals were so crammed full of things English and Fishbein wanted to cover that we barely had any fun. I almost wished English would put us through her stupid get-to-know-you exercises again, to lighten the mood. Almost.

I think she sensed our frustration, based on the big announcement she made in early October.

"I'll be gone for three weeks starting October seventeenth. My sister lives in Denmark, and I'm going over for her wedding."

"Three weeks? What about rehearsals? We'll get so behind," Kristina said.

"That's what I said, to no avail," whined Fishbein, for once siding with a student.

"Let me finish, please. I had always planned on this break in the rehearsal schedule. The show is coming along nicely, and if we stay on this path, we'll be fine for the show in mid-December. And, I have something else to occupy your time. You know how you all like to create your own shows?" We nodded but kept quiet. No one wanted to interrupt her. "We've decided to have a Senior Class Play for the first time. You get to write the show, produce and direct it, decide what it's about – everything. It's your baby." She opened her arms wide as if embracing us all.

"Sa-weet," sang Foster as the seniors cheered. Adrienne and I high fived.

October seventeenth couldn't come fast enough.

CHAPTER 10: "A PERSON'S A PERSON"

So many choices, so little time. Three weeks to create a show, start to finish. From scratch. Adrienne, Kristina, Foster, Ben, Emily, Sam and I crowded into the corner booth at TJ's Pizzeria and started talking about where to begin with the project. Alex and Adrienne's boyfriend Tom walked in with a crisp gust of air, Alex ignoring me as usual.

Everyone shifted to let them squeeze into the booth with us. Luckily, Alex sat a few people away from me and out of my direct line of vision, so it was easy to pretend he wasn't there.

"This is a huge gift, you guys, we have to make the most of it. I mean, we're finally free of that freaking control freak English and we can do what we want, when we want, how we want." I stopped, feeling awkward for my mini-leadership rant.

The awkwardness continued as people stared at me, or looked at each other and smirked.

"What? Did I miss something?"

"Let's keep going," Adrienne suggested.

"No, what? Why are you guys laughing?"

Foster reached across the table and took my hands, mock solemn. "Sadie, you know we love you. But honey, you are the biggest control freak we know. You might even put Ms. English to shame." A dagger pierced my lung. "But it's okay! That's why you're so good at theatre, and directing, and writing. Because you know what you want and how to get it. So don't worry about it."

I snuck a glimpse at Alex through the tears welling up in my eyes. The corner of his mouth twitched in a small, sympathetic movement. Or maybe he was holding in a smile, since he'd told me before I was only happy when I was in charge, but I refused to believe him.

"Look," Kristina said, pulling us back on track. "This has to be an original show, so forget about all the musicals we've wanted to do, like *Legally Blonde* and *Thirteen*." As she talked, I forced myself to focus on the show, not my character flaws. "Let's start with a theme. What should it be about?"

"It could be about some current event, like the war in Afghanistan. Or the impact of social media on our lives. Or something political, like a statement on the sad state of affairs in Washington, where the two sides can't get along enough to get anything done." Quiet Sam always shocked me with his interest in national politics. He casually pushed his long brown bangs out of his eyes as if we always talked about this sort of thing outside of class.

"We could do political satire. Like something from *The Colbert Report*," suggested Alex, making me squirm as I tried not to look at him.

"Satire would be awesome, but who do we want to make fun of?" Foster asked.

"Politicians," said Sam. Ben and Kristina said "no" at the same time.

"Boring," Foster added.

"Our parents?" asked Adrienne.

"Too easy. How about teachers?" I said. "I'd love to make fun of a few teachers."

Heads nodded.

"Yeah, and they'd have to let us, right? Since it's our play and all," said Ben.

Then we got stuck on how exactly to make fun of our teachers, and rambled off into conversation about things that bugged us, instead of people. Like having courses and subjects we hated forced down our throats. Like being treated like children by our parents even though we were off to college soon. Like being asked practically every day what we planned to do with the rest of our lives. Like dealing with teachers who actually made fun of the kids sometimes instead of protecting us. Like being made to feel like we didn't matter by pretty much any adult we dealt with. And worst of all, like not being listened to.

"A student's a person, so what if we're small," sang Adrienne softly, echoing a line in the song "Horton Hears A Who" from *Seussical*. Adrienne never sang, so everyone stopped talking and turned to her.

"What did you say?" Alex asked.

"You got the line wrong. It's 'a person's a person–'" Kristina tried to correct Adrienne but Alex talked over her.

"Sing it again, Adrienne," Alex encouraged.

"A student's a person, so what if we're small?" Adrienne asked uncertainly, scrunching her eyebrows together.

Alex and I looked at each other and grinned. Catching ourselves, we quickly looked away but kept grinning.

"I know what we can doo-oo," I gloated, in that obnoxious know-it-all voice we all hate but is so fun to use once in a while. "The answer's staring us in the face."

"Let's make a spoof of *Seussical*!" Alex practically yelled. How dare he steal my thunder? But it played well with our supposed break-up when I flashed him a dirty look, for real. I pushed my way back into the conversation before he took all the credit.

"This is what we wanted in the first place - to adapt *Seussical* into something of our own, but English wouldn't let us. So let's do it with our play. We can make fun of the teachers and maybe some other adults, too. Think about it. Horton and Gertrude and JoJo are all little people in a way, even though JoJo and the Whos and everyone living on the speck in Whoville are the only *really* little people. But they're all being crushed and judged and told what to do by Mayzie and the Sour Kangaroo and Yertle the Turtle and even the Cat in the Hat." I stopped for breath.

"And in Whoville, Mr. and Mrs. Mayor and General Schmitz are annoying adults too," added Foster. "I'm liking this." He shimmied his shoulders to emphasize the point.

"Awesome, let's do it," Ben said. "We can re-write the song lyrics easy, with all our experience at that."

"I love it. We'll make it an indictment of adult control over teenagers. So first, we need to pin down the story. How are we going to adapt it? Oh my God, we have so much to do!" exclaimed Kristina. "Let's get writing. Sadie, do you want to start and then I can be your editor? You know, just to keep things moving since we don't have lots of time," she offered. "Like a sounding board."

We were off and running. Within days, we'd made some big decisions. The show would be a one-act play, a condensed version of the original, as that was all we had time to produce. We thought about using modern pop songs for music like we'd done with the past two shows, but decided to keep the *Seussical* music because it would be faster and we had to admit we actually liked the songs.

The truth was, I had decided Stephen Flaherty, who wrote the music for *Seussical*, was a genius. A lot of musicals have too many songs that are important for telling the story but lame as songs. Not *Seussical*. Even short connecting pieces like "Egg, Nest & Tree" were catchy and fun for the actors and the audience.

We would only use a few of his songs in the Senior Class Play, so the show didn't get too long. We would tell as much of the story as we could through song, like a rock opera.

Plot-wise, we would keep the main story line of people not believing Horton, and people generally dissing Horton because he's different or slow, and ultimately being proven wrong. The plot-lines of Horton and Gertrude falling in love, and Gertrude finding out looks aren't everything, we would keep if they worked out, but they weren't mandatory to our satire.

The nice characters would be teenagers and the obnoxious, mean, close-minded characters would be adults. Naturally.

We were going to riff on the *Seussical* name and give the bad grown-up characters names that ended in -sical, things like Pop-sical for Mr. Mayor and Prin-sical for our new character making fun of Principal Zowicki. The teen characters' names would be similar to the real ones – Morton for Horton, Joey for JoJo, and Mildred for Gertrude, since it was the ugliest old-fashioned name we could think of.

Most important, it would be a modern adaptation of the story, set in our school in our time.

Amazingly, Kristina was actually helpful with the scripting. Working at my house one day, we decided that having an alternate universe like Whoville was too tricky and totally unrealistic, so we merged the Who characters into Morton's world. Kristina, Adrienne and I sat on my living room floor, loose pages of script and a big bowl of popcorn between us.

"But if we don't have mini-people living on a speck, what's going to be the thing that no one believes Horton about?" Adrienne asked.

"It could be anything at all – something he totally believes in, but no one else does," murmured Kristina in her thinking voice.

"Let's stick to our theme of grown-ups not believing teenagers or treating them like real people," I murmured back, reflexively matching Kristina's thinking voice. I thought about Fishbein and how annoying she was. I tried to focus on the bad teachers at Crudup, like Mr. Rooney the Phys Ed teacher who ridiculed the less athletic students during fitness testing every year. Or how frustrating it was when teachers assigned you a side in a debate based on what letter your last name started with, or what part of the room you sat in, instead of letting you pick the side you agreed with.

But my mind kept slipping over to Alex and everything he was going through. He was frustrated everywhere he turned, by EMTs and doctors who treated him like a kid, to police officers who wouldn't tell him anything about his own mother. I wondered how Mrs. Holman was feeling today, and how the lawyer was doing clearing her of the hospital drug theft charge. Why hadn't they found the person who actually did it?

"What about a mistaken identity plot line?" I asked. Adrienne and Kristina waited. "Morton could be accused of a crime he didn't do, like, say, painting graffiti on the school."

"And the adults refuse to believe he's innocent, even though they don't have proof," Kristina said.

"Or, since Joey's the creative one, he's accused of doing the graffiti and Morton's the only one who believes he's innocent?" Adrienne offered.

I smiled at her. Collaboration wasn't always a bad thing. "I think we've got it."

With the basic story line done, we talked casting at our next rehearsal. That was a nightmare. No one agreed on anything, and everyone wanted the best roles. Tom saved the day.

"We haven't actually picked a director yet, and someone has to be in charge," he pointed out. We were in my living room reading through the script to find weak spots. Alex had walked in and acted surprised to find us there. He'd been mostly quiet, though, and hung around the edges of the room, as if he were uncomfortable in my home.

"Clearly, I should be the director," Lucey said, triggering a small reflexive grunt of pain in my throat. "What?" she said in response to our stares. "I've been in CDC since the beginning, and I'm really good at being in charge. Look at how good I run the cheerleading squad."

"No offense, Luce, but I am Student Council President, and that job takes a lot more organization and leadership skills than cheerleading captain," Kristina said confidently.

"What about Sadie?" Adrienne asked quietly but firmly. "She was assistant director last year, after all."

Bickering ensued. I watched mutely as people chose sides between Lucey and Kristina. Adrienne gave up.

"Everyone, shut up!" Tom interrupted the chaos. "Holman should be the director. First of all, it sounds like Kristina and Lucey are *way* too busy with their other responsibilities." He managed not to laugh. "Second of all, Alex is the only one who's not in *Seussical*, so he has more time than us. And unlike most of you, he's capable of not playing favorites. Right, Alex?"

"Absolutely," Alex said, stepping into the middle of the room. "What's a favorite?"

CHAPTER II: THE BREAST PART

𝒜lex told me on the bus he was glad to be directing, because he needed more things to keep him from obsessing about his mother. Between school, soccer and now the Senior Class Play, he was trying to fill up every minute of every day. Any down time he spent holed up in Jesse's room studying, or at friends' houses, since we weren't allowed to hang. I was psyched he was directing, because we'd actually get to be in the same room once in a while.

He started making decisions left and right. One of the first was to not hold auditions. We didn't really have time. He got up to speed on the show by reading the *Seussical* script and our draft script. Then he cast the show. Just like that.

"I tried to be fair by giving the people who haven't had big roles in CDC or who don't have big roles in *Seussical* good parts in this one – especially the guys – so those of you who are used to having the lead, get ready to chill," he said, making almost everyone in the auditorium nervous. "Here's the cast list. There's a rehearsal schedule on the back. Time to get serious." Man. Give the guy a bullhorn and whip, why don't we?

He'd shown me the cast list the day before, and asked for advice, so I had to pretend to be as surprised as everyone else when we read through the casting at school. I waited to see if anyone would question why Alex wanted to act opposite me, but no one cared. We'd sweated that one, really wanting to be onstage together, but not wanting people to think we liked each other again. But casting often put strange couples together, and everyone was used to that.

SENIOR CLASS PLAY - SEUSSICAL SPOOF

Cast of Characters

KIDS

Morton (Horton):   Sam

Mildred (Gertrude):   Lucey

Joey (JoJo):   Eddie

Narrator: Ben

ADULTS

Class-sical
(Bird Girl):   Jocelyn

Cop-sical: Foster
(Bird Girl)

Doc-sical: Adrienne
(Bird Girl)

Prin-sical: Emily

In-Betweenzy (Mayzie):   Kristina

Pop-sical (Mr. Mayor):   Alex

Mom-sical (Mrs. Mayor):   Sadie

Gen. Shark-sical: Jason

School Comm. Members: Lindsay, ???

"We need one more senior to be a School Committee member, or Ben you can double up since the Narrator's a pretty small role," Alex said when we finished reading through the list.

"I think I can handle it," Ben said with a smirk and a nod.

"Hey, Alex? Thanks for giving me and Eddie such good roles," Sam said. He still seemed surprised that we'd forgiven him for last spring's issues.

"Why do I have the same role in both shows?" Jocelyn asked, wrinkling her freckled nose.

"Because you're stu–" started Lindsay.

"Because you're the perfect Bird Girl, and Alex knew you'd be the perfect teacher-slash-bird-girl, too," Tom the tactful chimed in. Jocelyn shrugged, satisfied.

Tom was going to lead stage crew for the show. Actually, he *was* the stage crew. We were going with a minimalist set and props to make things easy. We'd convinced Adrienne to come out from behind the curtain for the Senior Class Play. She agreed as long as she didn't have many speaking or solo singing lines. I couldn't wait to see her in the doctor role.

And then there was Lucey. My only problem with Alex's casting was the part of Mildred. I thought Kristina should get it. He insisted Lucey should have it, that a "nice girl" part would be good for her self-esteem. On some points, it was easy to pretend Alex and I were still fighting.

*B*y the next rehearsal, Lucey announced she'd written a solo for herself.

"We have to have this song. It's the perfect satire of Gertrude's tail feathers. If Gertrude was a person, she'd want bigger boobs."

"We haven't put the whole Mayzie-Gertrude bit in this play though. I don't know if we have time for another story line. Ms. English said to keep the play short."

"Sadie, it's not only your script. We all get a say." Lucey said, digging in.

"It could be pretty funny," Alex, the annoying director, said.

I glared at him, but inside I was already giving in. "I'm just afraid we won't be able to learn all this in time. We're pushing it as it is."

"I'll help you write new lines if you want," Kristina offered.

Alex knew how I felt about people interfering in my writing. "No, let Sadie do it." Kristina stared at him accusingly. "She is the scriptwriter after all. And we still get to suggest changes if we don't like it." Kristina nodded in surrender.

"Okay, Lucey let's hear it," Alex said.

Lucey didn't bother with the iPod. She started singing the short song *a cappella*, her powerful voice surprisingly restrained, in keeping with Mildred's personality.

<u>The World's Smallest Boobs on Miss Mildred McBuff</u>
(based on "The One Feather Tail of Miss Gertrude McFuzz")

```
DO DO, DO DO, DO DO, DO DO DO DO
I AM JUST A PLAIN GIRL
NAMED MILDRED MCBUFF
AND IT'S CLEAR TO ME
WHAT I'VE GOT'S NOT ENOUGH
MY HAIR'S DRAB AND BORING,
HOW FLAT IS MY CHEST?
THE BOYS DON'T LOOK PAST THAT,
THEY DON'T SEE THE REST

I RUB THEM. I WORK OUT.
EVEN TRIED GETTING FAT.
WHATEVER I DO,
I'M STILL FLATTER THAN FLAT.
I'M OUT OF IDEAS,
I CAN'T TELL WRONG FROM RIGHT.
```

```
A BOD THAT NEVER BRINGS ME JOY
WON'T EVER CATCH ME A NICE BOY
THE WORLD'S SMALLEST BOOBS
THAT I'M STUCK WITH FOR LIFE
```

Lucey looked offended when we started giggling while she sang, probably thinking we were laughing because she had the biggest chest of all the girls at Crudup. She pumped up her volume to be heard over our laughs. But by the time she finished and we were practically rolling in the aisles, she understood that our reaction was a compliment and that we thought the song was funny, not her. Already, I was thinking we could strap her chest in for the early scenes and let it loose when she had a boob job to impress Morton, 'cause clearly that's where this was going.

"I guess that settles that," Alex said, practically crying. "'The World's Smallest Boobs on Miss Mildred McBuff' is in the show."

CHAPTER 12: SIBLING-LIKE RIVALRY

"Sadie wrote this one," Alex said at our next rehearsal, sounding a little too proud. I glared at him. He cleared his throat. "Let's see if it's any good." He passed around sheets of paper with my lyrics on them.

"It's based on 'Solla Sollew', which has to be one of the prettiest *Seussical* songs," I said, while searching on YouTube for the video. No *a cappella* singing for me. "I'm picturing Morton on one side of the stage, Joey on the other, not really friends but together in their anguish. The ensemble is upstage, singing background vocals."

"Just pick one, there's like eight videos of the song there," Jocelyn whined, watching me scroll through the YouTube options.

"It has to be a regular *Seussical* version to match. The *Seussical, Jr.* one is different," I said, finally picking one of the videos. "Okay, this is the one. Here we go."

I looked down at my lyric sheet rather than watch people's expressions as they followed along. Thankfully, Foster and then others started singing along with me.

<u>A Place for Me</u>
(based on "Solla Sollew",
new lyrics by Sadie Perkins)
start at 0:58 into the video)

Morton

Why do they all hate me, I just don't understand
What did i do to offend them
They laugh at me, Don't they know that i am
A person through and through
I have feelings too.
A place for me, A place for me

Chorus

A place for me, A place for me

(skip the spoken parts of original song.)
(lights up on joey at his school dorm desk.)

Joey

There's a much better place, That i know in my
heart
Somewhere that's not on my atlas

Joey & morton

If i can find it, I won't fall apart
For there i'll be free. A place for me.

Morton

I just want that one friend, Who'll like me for me
One who will stay by my side

Chorus

A place for me

Joey
I just want to be me, To live my own life

Joey & morton
My way wrong or right

Chorus
My way wrong or right

Joey & morton
My way wrong or right

Joey
I don't like the weapons, The army, the war
Fighting is not in my nature

Morton
Can't they just leave me, And mock me no more

Joey & morton
I'll go far away. Forget the things they say

All
And i'll be on my way

A place for me, a place for me (repeat 3 times)
A place for me

Joey & morton
I'm lonely, can't you see

Chorus
A place for me

"Someone kill me now, I'm so depressed," joked Lindsay.

"It's not really satire, is it?" said Kristina. "I mean, because the words are new but the theme is like *Solla Sollew*," she said, answering her own question. "But I love it, I mean, it's fine, it will work. And we had to change the words anyway, didn't we." She smiled weakly.

"It's perfect, Sadie, don't listen to them," Foster reassured me. "I vote it on the island."

"Okay, it's in," Alex said definitively. After reminding people we needed more songs stat, he ran us through our lines.

"How come Joey's parents are the only ones who talk in Seuss-speak?" Lucey interrupted Scene 4 to ask.

"Seuss-speak?" Jocelyn asked.

"You know, rhyming, like Dr. Seuss books," Lucey explained.

"I don't have time to write the entire thing in rhyme, so I just did the Joey and his parents scenes that way," I said.

Lucey scoffed. "I thought she was supposed to be good at this," she said *sotto voce t*o Jocelyn.

"I– It's– It's not that easy," I gurgled while screaming inside.

"It really isn't, Luce," Kristina said in my defense. "I tried some and it's tougher than it looks. Plus, it will take longer to memorize all that rhyming and we don't have a lot of time. If we're talking regular and we screw up a line, it won't be as noticeable."

Lucey eyed her friend like she was a traitor. She opened her mouth, to say something else biting I'm sure, but Alex pre-empted.

"Lucey, let's work with what we've got, and if you want to try writing some of the regular lines in rhyme, go for it and I'll look at them."

She gave in to Alex, like he knew she would. She still owed him for last year. With the diva under control, we moved on.

"Alex, your pancakes are getting cold," my mother yelled up the stairs. Since Alex moved in, she'd been making even more effort to cook breakfast, as if a warm meal made it okay that Mrs.

Holman was in the hospital fighting a deadly disease with no end in sight.

Alex's heavy footsteps thumped down the stairs.

"Coming, Mrs. Perkins," he said, breathing slightly heavily and using his fingers to comb his damp hair, which looked almost brown. "Sorry I'm late, but I had to wait for the bathroom. Again," he said grumpily, squinting his eyes at me briefly before flashing a resigned smile at my mother.

"Hey, I have a morning beauty routine that I've had for years. Jesse could handle it. Why can't you?" I didn't mention that my morning routine took longer now that he lived in my house. It was a royal pain worrying how I looked every second, but I couldn't walk around with no make-up and icky hair and sweats with my boyfriend nearby, now could I? I even had to shave my legs and pits more often.

"Seems to me you're both taking a lot of time in the bathroom these days," Mom said, surprising me. Was she onto us? "I know you want to look your best for your classmates, but it is only school you're going to." More likely, she thought we were trying to get new dates. She seemed to be buying our charade of being broken up.

"I'll try to go faster," Alex said, sucking up big time. Stabbing and picking up an entire pancake, he turned to me. "And do you think you could clean your hair out of the sink from now on? It's kind of gross," he said, and tore off half the pancake with his teeth.

"Really. I was here first, you know."

"Sadie," Mom warned from across the table.

"Well, Mom, I finally got the bathroom to myself when Jesse left for college, but now I have to change my life again, and start cleaning out the sink every time I brush my hair? It's not fair," I whined, pleased with my acting.

"A nice sister would have been doing that all along," Alex said. "You probably never saw Jesse's hair in the sink. And you don't see mine."

"Please. Your hair is like two or three inches long. Even if it was in the sink, I probably wouldn't notice it."

"Both of you, just stop it," Mom said, clanking her fork down. "Honestly, it's like having siblings in the house again. You will both co-exist under this roof, peaceably, from now on. Understood?" She shifted her glare back and forth between us. "I can't hear you," she hissed.

"Yes, Mrs. Perkins."

"Yes, Mom."

(SADIE and ALEX settle into their
regular seats on the school bus. SADIE
laughs.)

SADIE

That was great. I wanted to write down
some of our lines to use in a script
someday. Definitely one of our better
performances.

ALEX

Performance? Who was acting? You really
do take a long time in the bathroom and
leave hair in the sink.

(SADIE stares at him until he looks at
her.)

But I'm not mad or anything. I was just
pretending to be mad. But it's funny how
real life can give you ideas for the
acting, don't you think?

SADIE

Hm. You worried me for a minute there.
Sometimes I'm not sure when you're
acting and when you're really annoyed
with me. I wish we had more normal time
than just this bus ride.

                    ALEX

Me too. The longer we do this, the
harder it's getting.

(They sigh in unison.)

                    SADIE

Fourteen minutes a day isn't enough time
to be ourselves. I thought I liked
acting but this is brutal. There must be
a way we can keep our secret and still
find some time together.

                    ALEX

I know, but have you noticed your
parents sleep with their door open all
the time now?

(SADIE nods.)

So we can't slip away at night to talk.

(ALEX sighs.)

We'll think of something. But back to
your house, I don't think it's healthy
to pretend to be mad at each other so
much. Kato doesn't like it either.

(They look at each other and smile
weakly.)

Do you think we could be a little
friendlier without your mom getting
suspicious?

                    SADIE

I think we have to ease up. I mean, she
basically told us we have to. We just
have to get the balance right.

Friendlier, but not too friendly. That's what worries me.

                    ALEX

What do you mean?

                    SADIE

(Swallows.)

I worry that if we ease up, how we really feel is going to show.

(ALEX squints his gorgeous green eyes at SADIE, waiting. She inhales deeply.)

Alex, I have a hard time being near you and pretending we're not going out. I feel like there's electricity or something between us and I can't believe everyone else doesn't feel it.

(Looks into her lap for security. ALEX takes her hand.)

                    ALEX

Hey. Me too. I thought it was just me.

(They sit, holding hands, until the bus stops at school.)

CHAPTER 13: REUNITED

"*T*his was a really tough song to do," Kristina said, widening her eyes in awe of her own lyric-writing capabilities. "It changes tempo a hundred times and you have to cram a lot of words into it."

"So why don't we skip it if it's so hard? We said we weren't using every song," Jocelyn said, unhelpfully, scanning her silky black hair and ruby lips in a compact mirror.

Kristina looked at Jocelyn like she were a child. The exact behavior we were condemning in our play, I thought, but it was different between friends. It was okay for us to give each other a hard time and make fun of our friends, since we were all in the same shaky boat on the same unpredictable waters.

"It's a really important part of the play, when we show that the adults are blaming Joey and Morton for the graffiti, even without any evidence. It's kind of critical to the rest of the story," Kristina explained. "We have to use it."

"Plus, it's a great all-cast number," I pointed out.

"Yeah, 'cause our thirteen-person cast is going to be so impressive," said Foster.

I wasn't sure if he was joking, but it didn't matter. Thirteen was what we had, and it had to be enough. And all-cast numbers were mandatory in musicals.

Kristina pulled up a YouTube video of "Biggest Blame Fool" on the computer in the "office" nook next to her kitchen, where six of us were squeezed together. We followed along on the lyrics she'd given us, Kristina singing her new words to "World's Biggest Fool" along with the video to help us match them up.

"It keeps getting stuck on the line 'world's biggest fool at the Smalltown High School'," I said when the song was over. "It's a lot of consonants to spit out. But it would sound worse saying 'biggest fool at Smalltown High School' without the 'the'."

"Do we have to use Smalltown?" asked Emily, pushing a chunk of frizzy dark brown hair behind her ear. "I mean, I know it's part of the joke, making fun of our own town, but I agree with Sadie – it's not flowing right."

Since Emily hardly ever spoke up and had a crappy, sympathy-inducing home life, when she did make a suggestion, she usually got her way. So after tossing around ideas, we changed the name from Smalltown High School to Dominion High School. Dominion seemed to fit with the theme of adults dominating the kids.

"Wait – I'll re-print them," Kristina said when she saw me crossing out Smalltown on my lyric sheet. "Let me just find and replace the Smalltowns," she murmured while clicking away on the keyboard.

"Kristina, don't waste the paper," Adrienne admonished but paper was already spewing out of the printer.

"Let's try it again. It's a tricky song," Kristina said, passing around the fresh pages. "Remember, we start on the line 'Why that speck is as small as the head of a pin.'"

WORLD'S BIGGEST FOOL
(to the tune of "Biggest Blame Fool")
Lyrics by Kristina Kent

(skip original opening lines; start when the original says
"why that speck is as small as the head of a pin")

(Class-sical, spoken, to Joey)
I can't believe you did that, what are you -- crazy?
You've lost it now, Joey, that's plain to see
(laughs)
(sung)
You're the world's biggest fool at Dominion High School
And everyone agrees
The world's biggest fool at Dominion High School
Yeah, everyone can see
Some say you're lazy, some say un-cool
You're the world's biggest fool at Dominion High School

(Morton, spoken)
But wait, wait a second - it's not hard to see
He should be innocent 'til proven guilty
How can you blame him when you've got no proof?
We live in America - we live by the truth!

(Cop-sical)
Listen to Morton, why does he even care?
Maybe we should take a closer look there

(Adults)
Oh he's the world's biggest fool at Dominion High School
And everybody knows
The world's biggest fool at Dominion High School

(Cop-sical)
He's a jerk

(Class-sical)
He's dense

(Doc-sical)
He's slow

(Cop-sical)
Morton tries hard but this is the truth
He's the world's biggest fool at Dominion High School
'cause you're in trouble now, you're in trouble now
You're in trouble now

(Adults)
Big fool at Dominion High School

(Cop-sical)
You're in trouble now, trouble now, you're in trouble now

(Adults)
Big fool at Dominion High School

(Prin-sical enters, sees people bothering Morton)
What the heck do my eyes see?
Oh please, let that Morton be!

(Adults except Prin-sical)
Wanna hear? Wanna hear? Wanna wanna hear?

(Class-sical)
Through the hallways the gossip flew

(Adults except Prin-sical)
Wanna hear? Wanna hear? Wanna wanna hear?

(Doc-sical)
He says Joey's innocent, he's gone crazy too

(Prin-sical's tone changes. Clearly displeased with Morton,
she adopts the tone of a teacher in front of a class.)
Our lesson today: why one should not tell lies.
Whaddya says, folks, is Morton telling a lie?

(cut spoken cat section from original.)

(Adults)
World's biggest fool at Dominion High School

(Mildred)
I'm Mildred McBuff and this boy I adore
He's always been normal and still is i'm sure

(Adults)
World's biggest fool at Dominion High School

(Mildred)
You all should believe him and not be so blind
Can't you be like him? Can't you be kind?

(Adults)
Wanna hear? Wanna hear? Wanna wanna hear?

(In-Betweenzy enters.)
My name's In-Betweenzy, I'm eighteen years old

(Adults)
Wanna hear? Wanna hear? Wanna wanna hear?

(In-Betweenzy)
Prin-sical expelled me, but why I don't know
Oh why, I don't know, I don't know
I don't know, I don't know!

(Adults, to Morton)
You're in trouble now, trouble now, you're in trouble now

(In-Betweenzy)
Big fool at Dominion High School

(Adults, to Joey)
You're in trouble now, trouble now, you're in trouble now

(In-Betweenzy)
Big fool at Dominion High School

(Morton)
I think I should help him, Because listen up,
A student's somebody, and you were one once
A student's somebody, and you were one --

(Adults)
World's biggest fool at Dominion High School

(Prin-sical)
Let the truth get in the way
Spinning tales, tellin' lies
Can't you see with your own eyes
What would your parents say?

(Doc-sical)
What story next are you gonna make up
That Morton's not thinkin' the same as us

(Adults)
World's biggest fool at Dominion High School
At Dominion High School
At Dominion High School

Dominion worked. We sang along to the song a few more times, pausing in a few spots to work out the timing of certain lines.

"This song rocks," Kristina gloated when we called it quits for the day and turned on *America's Next Top Model* to empty our full minds. She was right. Three songs down, three or four more to go.

"I'm so happy you guys aren't really broken up!" Adrienne said, a hugging jumping bean threatening to pull me over. Alex and I had decided to let Adrienne and Tom in on our secret so they could help us find time together and keep our sanity.

"Now the four of us can hang together like before. Yeah!" she said, stepping back and wrapping her arms around her torso to contain her excitement.

"Not exactly," I cautioned. "We can only be ourselves around you two, nobody else. If Dad hears a rumor at school, I'm dead and Alex will have to move out."

"Okay, got it," she said, getting serious. "So, how will this work?"

"Every now and then, I'll come visit you like today, and Alex can do something with Tom, and then they can just manage to end up here if your parents aren't home." Alex and I had worked out logistics on the bus that morning.

"Sweet. And you know they're never home 'til dinnertime. When's the first stealth meeting?"

Her doorbell rang. Anticipation radiated out of me.

"Let me guess. Now?"

*Y*ou know that feeling when you're dead tired and you climb into your own bed with your favorite blanket and the sheets are the perfect combination of soft and cool? That's what it was like hugging Alex for the first time in over a month. Sitting side by side and holding hands on the school bus once or twice a day was not enough.

By the time we finished hugging, Adrienne and Tom had left the room, leaving me and Alex alone, finally. We talked about everything we couldn't or wouldn't, or didn't have time to, in our fourteen minutes on the bus. How he was suffering over his mother's illness. How we were both freaking out about college decisions. And gossip like who sucked on the soccer team and the iron grip Ms. English kept on us at rehearsal.

I asked if people were still calling him TB Boy to his face and in true guy fashion he said he couldn't care less. He just laughed when I said only golden boy Alex could survive the threat of potentially, single-handedly infecting an entire school with a violent disease, and come out not only unscathed, but more popular than ever. Given his extreme unpopularity a few years ago, it was all pretty ironic.

I was sitting in his lap in an overstuffed armchair when Tom and Adrienne walked back in.

"You guys want to do something? Game? TV? Work on the show?" Adrienne asked.

"We have to stay here, right? We wouldn't want to be seen in public with you guys or anything. Yuck," Tom joked, grimacing.

We settled on the show option, gathering around Adrienne's computer to work on our finale based on *Seussical*'s "The People Versus Horton the Elephant". Another high-energy, frantic-paced number like "Biggest Blame Fool", it took all my concentration to make any progress on it. Eventually, Alex and I hit our lyric-writing rhythm, and soon we were working together like nothing had changed.

That night in bed, I smiled and re-played the afternoon in my head. Even the sound of Alex hacking up gross guy phlegm in the bathroom next to me couldn't ruin my warm fuzzy feeling. I slept like a girl with a great boyfriend.

CHAPTER 14: HYPHEN HELL

*W*ho-ssical. Who-sicle. Whossical. Hoosical.

At our next Senior Class Play rehearsal, we took a break from running the show to figure out what to call our original drama. Now that we had a whodunnit plot line – who was the graffiti vandal? – we had thought up the name *Who-ssical*, but were arguing about how to spell it.

"We're spending way too much time on this. I'm going to delegate the decision to..." Alex scanned the room, twice, and sighed. "I'm going to make this decision. Everyone who wants a vote, write down your choice and give it to me, and by tomorrow I'll let you know what spelling we're going with."

People nodded. It amazed me how no one argued with Alex as director. How come no one respected me like that when I was assistant director last year?

At least I knew I'd get my way with the name now.

"I wrote a killer song for Eddie," Foster said nobly, pulling up the YouTube video on the music room computer.

"It's based on 'It's Possible' and the Joey character sings it, right after his parents tell him they're sending him away to military school because he spends too much time thinking and on his computer and maybe he did the graffiti on the school, too. I think we should make it a little slower than the original version."

It's Happening . . . . Joey

Based on "It's Possible" from Seussical
New lyrics by Foster Cordeiro

(Slower than original.)

What are they doing, they don't know how I feel
I really mean it when I say it's for real
I love to create things, the computer's my tool
I'll be a designer, not somebody's fool
It's possible. Isn't it possible?

With monsters and dragons, or maybe a queen
Historical figures come to life on my screen
Designing a world way beyond this old house
I make what I want when I pick up my mouse
It's possible. Isn't it possible?
It's possible. Isn't it possible?

But they want to send me so far far away
Where no one will care that I want to create
There'll be no place for color
I'll stay, I'll stay in the lines

(cut 1:30 – 2:20, the interlude/dance and beach
boy-type song)

I want them to luv me, so what can I do
Change who I am and be good thru and thru
I'll go to that school where you do what they say
And no one has fun in the night or the day
It's happening. Clearly it's happening.
It's happening. Clearly it's happening.
It's happening.
Clearly it's, clearly it's happening.

"Foster, that's perfect for right after the first scene with Joey and his parents," I said.

"Duh, Sade, like I said," Foster said, but his wrinkled brow quickly disappeared and he grinned, and I knew he was happy that I liked his lyrics. "Eddie, want me to teach it to you?" Foster asked.

When things were going Foster's way, he couldn't be more helpful. He had a duet and a pretty big part as Mr. Mayor in *Seussical*, and the role he wanted in *Who-ssical* as the cop. The policeman was loosely based on the Sour Kangaroo role, which meant Foster would get to let loose with some Aretha Franklin-style singing in our Senior Class Play. So this year, things were definitely going Foster's way.

And mine, I realized with a shock. Mayzie in *Seussical* and acting opposite Alex in *Who-ssical*. Just what I wanted. Every other show, either Foster or I was comforting the other for not getting the right role. Until this moment, I hadn't realized how lucky I was. The thought echoed one of my solos in *Seussical*, the "How Lucky You Are" reprise, which for some reason cracked me up, making my friends stare at me like I was a lunatic.

"It's nothing," I said in answer to their looks. "Let's keep going."

"What do you mean, you're not sure you want to spell it with a hyphen? You have to use the hyphen or people won't know how to pronounce it," I protested.

Alex and I were sitting at Adrienne's kitchen table. From the corner of my eye, I saw Adrienne slink out of the room.

"Sadie, there can be more than one right way, you know," Alex said, irritation creeping into his voice.

"I know, and my way is one of them," I said, scribbling Whossical on the paper on the table, and then Who-ssical. "Look at it. Seriously, Alex, if you don't use the hyphen, people might think it's called *Woss-i-cal* or *Hoss-i-cal*. You need to set off the word *Who* with the hyphen." How could he not see this?

"I just think it looks weird with a hyphen then two s's." He wasn't giving up. "I think *Whossical* with no hyphen works best."

He stared me down, then played his trump card. "And I'm the director, so I get to decide."

"Man, we could have had this conversation at home. It would have fit right in with our fighting roles," I said, knowing I'd lost. It wasn't even worth reminding him that I was the scriptwriter.

"But listen, I am going to take your other suggestion," he said, trying to make peace.

I raised an eyebrow but stayed silent and refused to look at him.

"I like your idea of calling it *Whossical: The Seussical The Musical Spoof.* That's pretty funny." He stood in front of me so I had to see him. "And it gives it some context, you know, saying that it's a satire and that it's based on *Seussical.* So I'm going to use that." He bent over so his head was level with mine but I continued staring into space. "Okay?" he asked, moving his head directly in front of my face so I had no choice but to focus on him. I laughed.

"Okay. Fine." I laughed again. "Fine!" I said, pushing him back so I could stand up too. "Now, we better go. My dad said dinner's early tonight."

"Remember," Alex said, grabbing his backpack. "Don't be *too* friendly at your house. Now that we're being sort of nice to each other again, I feel like your parents are watching us every second."

"I know, right? We might need to fake break up *again*, just so they don't worry," I said, pulling my hoodie off the back of the kitchen chair.

$\mathcal{M}$y parents casually sat down on our living room couch, one on either side of me. My stomach sank lower than the flowered cushion I sat on. Kato padded out of the room, tail between his legs, the traitor.

"Um, hi?" I said, pretending to return my attention to *Cabaret* on the TV.

"How do you think this Alex situation is going?" Mom – never one for beating around the bush – asked, as her blue eyes bored into the side of my head.

So many answers to that one. "What do you mean?" I hedged, shifting to face her.

"I mean, him living here and all. Because his mother's doctor thinks she's going to be in the hospital for quite a while. They're having real problems finding a treatment she'll respond to, and they don't dare let her go home until the TB is under control. They were thinking of moving her to a bigger hospital but it looks like a specialist is going to come see her at the Dayton hospital instead."

"Oh. That stinks. I mean, except the specialist part. That's good," I said, mentally kicking myself because I hadn't asked Alex about his mom in a few days. I knew he thought about her constantly. But we had so little time to ourselves that I didn't always remember to ask about Mrs. Holman.

"You and Alex seem to be doing...okay with the situation," Dad chipped in, making me swivel to face him on the other side. "And I hear you're sitting together on the school bus these days."

It took all my self-control to keep my face blank, while inside I marveled at the Crudup gossip machine. Why the hell would anyone mention me and Alex sitting together on the bus, to someone else at school, in a place where my father could overhear them?

"Um, Dad, you know I don't have any friends on my bus. And it's lame enough to have to even ride the bus. If I didn't sit with Alex, I'd be even more lame because I'd look friendless." He nodded, unconvinced. "If it makes you feel better, we don't talk to each other. We just listen to our iPods."

"Anyway," he said, taking off his rimless glasses and rubbing the bridge of his nose, "we were a little worried at first, because you two seemed so angry with each other. I'm sure it was hard with him moving in so soon after you two broke up." He was doing a good job pretending to understand teenage romance. Mom must have coached him.

I made a non-committal noise.

"So, we're glad you two are getting along better now." He cleared his throat. I waited.

"And?" I prompted.

Mom cleared her throat. Wow. "And, we just want to make sure that you're not getting along *too* well. Because we couldn't in good conscience let Alex stay here if you two were dating again. It wouldn't be appropriate."

I tilted my head down and peered up at her with incredulous eyes, using her favorite gesture. For fun, I cleared my throat.

"Let me get this straight. You want me and Alex to be friends, but not more than friends. Is that right?"

Dad's voice made me turn back to him. His unruly salt-and-pepper hair was now sticking up in a few places. "You don't really even have to be friends, if that's too complicated. We'd rather have you not be friends than be too good friends. You know." He glanced at my mother and made a face. "What? It's the truth."

"So, even though Alex is my oldest friend, and has been my best friend for years, you guys would rather have us not talking at all, then talking too much?"

"Well, if it's just talking we're talking about, I don't think we care so much–" Dad started but trailed off after looking at my mother again.

"Do you know how twisted that sounds? That you don't want me to get along with my best friend? What exactly is it you do want?" I was finding it easy to stand up to them since I was playing a role. Or maybe it was their own weak preparation that made it easier. I actually felt like I had the upper hand for once.

Mom sighed. "I think we should just carry on as we are and pretend this conversation never happened," she said, standing up. Dad quickly copied her. "But Sadie, seriously, if you and Alex should get romantically involved again, I would expect you to tell me," she said, cutting to the chase. "Deal?"

Thankfully, she kept talking, not waiting for a response. "And, by the way, a woman from the Department of Child Services is coming by in a while, so I need you to be around."

I swallowed the small gasp in my throat. "Really? Why?"

"They say it's just a formality, but I'm a little nervous that they want to take Alex from us. With no cure in sight for Jenny, they're butting in and making noises that maybe this isn't the best environment for him." My mothers' shoulders slumped lower and lower as she spoke.

"Why would they think that?"

"I don't know. That's what we're going to find out." She turned to go but quickly turned back. "And Sadie, she may want to talk to you."

"Me? Why?" A vision of being strapped into a hard metal chair, sweating under bright interrogation lights, flitted through my head.

"Again, I don't know. But be on your best behavior. Obviously."

*T*wo hours later, I sat down in front of Ms. Duncan from the Massachusetts DCS. No bare metal chair or blinding lights, but why had I never noticed how hard it was to get comfortable in my own kitchen chair?

She was youngish, maybe thirty, with smooth milk chocolate colored skin and a tight Afro. A snug, beige blazer and skirt encased her slender frame. Her smile was friendly, but her eyes were weary steel.

MS. DUNCAN

Okay, Sadie, this won't take long. I just have a few questions for you.

(Sadie nods.)

How do you like having Alex living in your house?

SADIE

Um, it's fine. I guess.

(Bites her lip while Mrs. Duncan waits.)

So, it's kind of like having a brother around again, not that I need one. I mean, I love my real brother Jesse, but it was kind of nice having the bathroom to myself when he left for college. So I miss that. But I guess it's okay. Having Alex here.

MS. DUNCAN

(Cocks her head this way and that, studying Sadie.)

Are you two good friends?

SADIE

(Looking away.)

Friends? Us? No way. I mean, not really. I mean, we travel in different circles. He's a jock. I'm a thespian.

(Looks at Ms. Duncan.)

I'm into theatre. Drama.

(Ms. Duncan nods condescendingly. Sadie kicks herself mentally. Of course Ms. Duncan knows what thespian means. Note to self: Control rambling.)

MS. DUNCAN

And because you, <u>travel in different circles</u>, you don't interact much at school or socially?

(Sadie nods, pleased.)

That must be difficult in such a small school. Surely you run into him from time to time, or have some classes together.

(Sadie swallows hard, hoping Ms. Duncan doesn't notice.)

And the other kids must know he's living here. Is that hard for you? Do they talk? You know, spread rumors?

(Ms. Duncan waves her hands as she talks. Sadie stares at the hands, mesmerized, then shakes her head a little as if waking herself up.)

SADIE

It's not like that. Everyone knows what's going on with Alex's mother, so they're just glad he didn't have to move out of town, 'cause the soccer team really needs him. That's what I hear. From the soccer people.

(Sadie's eyes twitch as she stifles a wince.)

MS. DUNCAN

Still, it must feel strange having a classmate living with you.

SADIE

(Waits. Waits some more.)

I'm sorry. Was that a question?

MS. DUNCAN

Never mind. So, it doesn't bother you to have Alex staying here. And you're not really friends even though you're classmates in a very small school.

(Narrows her eyes ever so slightly.)

And I'm sure you two have never <u>dated</u> or anything, since you don't even travel in the same circles.

(Looks Sadie up and down. Sadie wills her face to remain blank while establishing in her head a character who would never date Alex Holman.)

SADIE

Trust me, we have never dated. And never will. I mean look at him. Why would someone that cute be interested in me?

(Ms. Duncan stares at Sadie for an eternity, then nods to the side ever so slightly. Sadie's heart threatens to beat right out of her chest.)

Can I say something, Ms. Duncan?

MS. DUNCAN

By all means.

SADIE

It's just that, even though Alex and I aren't friends, it would be horrible to make him leave Crudup High his senior year. This is a really big year for us. For all the seniors, I mean. And he needs to finish up his education where it started. Right here. I think. It's only fair.

MS. DUNCAN

Hmm. Tell that to my boss. As far as I'm concerned, Alex is almost eighteen and a legal adult, and there are a lot of other kids out there who need my help more than him.

Thank you, Sadie. That's all I need.

As I left the kitchen, legs shaking, I congratulated myself on my performance. I may have failed on the honesty front, but I'd played my character well. And my character had lied to protect a friend, so it was okay.

CHAPTER 15: PREMATURE JUDGEMENT

*D*oubts threatened to derail the *Whossical* dress rehearsal. Finally, we were in control of our destiny, and we were freaking out.

Would we get in trouble for making fun of the teachers and other authority figures?

Could we get away with saying damn and boobs?

Were two entire songs about breasts crossing the line?

Running through our first number did nothing to quell our doubts. Sam and Eddie had re-written "Horton Hears A Who" as a pretty good introduction to the main characters, but a scathing portrait of the adult characters.

```
Judging . . . . . . . . . . . . . .All
        (based on "Horton Hears A Who")

(Ensemble except Prin-sical wander onto
stage in small groups while singing.)

                ADULTS

    TOO TOO FUNNY
    TOO TOO TOO FUNNY FUNNY
    TOO TOO FUNNY
    TOO TOO TOO FUNNY FUNNY

    (REPEAT)

            CLASS-SICAL

    OH WE ARE THE ADULTS
    AT DOMINION HIGH SCHOOL
```

WE'LL TELL YOU WHO'S HERE
LOTS OF KIDS SO UNCOOL

COP-SICAL

FIRST THERE'S MORTON

ADULTS

MORTON!

COP-SICAL

FRIENDS WITH NOBODY ELSE
THAT MORTON THE FOOLISH ONE

ADULTS

MORTON THE FOOLISH ONE (REPEAT)

COP-SICAL

MORTON THE FOOLISH ONE
SHOULD STAY IN HIS SHELL

DOC-SICAL

AND THEN THERE IS JOEY
A STRANGE EMO BOY
WHO LIVES IN HIS ROOM
NEVER MAKING A NOISE

CLASS-SICAL

AND DON'T FORGET MILDRED
THE MOST AWKWARD OF ALL
WHAT'S UP WITH THESE KIDS TODAY
THEY'RE NOT NORMAL AT ALL

MORTON

I HEAR YOU

OTHER KIDS

SAID MORTON

MORTON

I HEAR WHAT YOU YELL
YOU ARE THE TEACHERS
YOU REALLY SHOULD HELP

MILDRED

BUT INSTEAD YOU MAKE FUN
AND YOU JUDGE US
ALL THE DAY

JOEY

(Spoken/Rapped)
OH MAN, THIS IS WRONG
OUR TEACHERS ARE MEAN
THEY'RE SUPPOSED TO BE HELPFUL
INSTEAD THEY DEMEAN

COULD IT REALLY BE REAL
COULD IT REALLY BE TRUE
OUR TEACHERS ALL HATE US
OH WHAT DO WE DO?

WE'VE GOT TO GET PAST THIS
THEY CAN'T RUN OUR LIVES
SO WHAT THEY DON'T LISTEN
ABOVE WE MUST RISE
IF WE'RE GOING TO GET THROUGH THIS

MORTON

(Singing)
YOU MAY NOT BELIEVE THIS
I AM NOT A DUNCE
A STUDENT'S SOMEBODY,
AND YOU WERE ONE ONCE
A STUDENT'S SOMEBODY,
AND YOU WERE ONE ONCE

```
                     ADULTS

        TOO TOO FUNNY
        TOO TOO TOO FUNNY FUNNY
        TOO TOO FUNNY
        TOO TOO TOO FUNNY FUNNY
        TOO TOO FUNNY FUNNY

        THEY TALK TIL THEY'RE BLUE
        WE DON'T HEAR WHAT THEY SAY
        WE'VE GOT OUR OWN LIVES
        AT THE END OF THE DAY
        THEY'RE NOT PEOPLE TO US
        THEY'RE A FAIL OR A PASS
        IT'S BETTER TO THINK THAT
        THAN GET CLOSE AND ATTACHED
```

"You know, they could have given us an advisor to make sure we didn't do anything we shouldn't," Jocelyn complained.

"Something tells me after they see our Senior Class Play, they might do that next year," Foster said, making us giggle nervously.

"Well, wait, though. It's not like anyone outside the school is going to come, except maybe our parents," rationalized Kristina. "It's mostly for the other students."

"And it's not like we're saying our teachers are as bad as these characters. It is a satire, after all. We should make sure that's really clear, though," I said.

"Good idea, Sadie," Adrienne said. "Let's add the definition of satire to the program. In the name of education," she joked.

"In the name of cover your ass," Foster said, making us laugh again.

CHAPTER 16: IT'S SHOWTIME (WHOSSICAL)

*F*riday night, there was no turning back. The tingles of anticipation that signaled show time smothered any remaining hesitation about the content of our show, at least for me. We had been given free rein by Ms. English, and we were going to use it.

At 7:37, the auditorium was two-thirds full of mostly students, plus some teachers and parents. I had casually suggested to my parents that they skip this show, but they didn't listen.

Alex walked in front of the curtain and welcomed everyone to *Whossical, the Seussical the Musical Spoof.*

"This is the first Senior Class Play at Crudup High. We came up with the concept, Sadie wrote the script, and everyone pitched in on lyrics. Tom 'the Man' Cole is in charge of Stage Crew and, well, it says who did what else in your program. This is a satire, so it's making some comments on things that bug us, but mostly it's meant to be fun. So, here goes. We hope you like it."

*A*s Alex leaves the stage, Tom dims the lights and the students in the audience whoop and holler. Tom blasts "Another Brick in the Wall: Part II" from the sound system, setting a rebellious tone for our satire as Pink Floyd and a bunch of young kids sing about not needing education. From backstage, I hear some of the kids in the audience singing along to the chorus.

As the song fades out, Tom slowly brings up the stage lights and the ensemble strolls on, "adults" from stage left, "teens" from stage right. Patrick, an eighth grade piano whiz discovered by Tom, drums out the mildly tribal introduction to "Horton Hears A Who" or, in our version, "Judging". Not our best title idea but we ran out of time and it gets the point across.

Class-sical, Cop-sical, and Doc-sical move upstage. From the wings where I'm peeking between our patched curtains, I see how self-conscious Adrienne looks as Doc-sical.

"Too, too funny, too too too funny funny," the adults sing, instead of "who who wah dah" like in *Seussical*. Foster and even Jocelyn are pros at onstage singing, so they enunciate and convey their lines clearly in the introduction. I hold my breath waiting to see how Adrienne does.

"And then there is Joey, a strange emo boy," she sings, and continues attacking Joey. She did it! She was loud enough, and pretty clear. I'm so proud of my mean-acting little friend.

The audience is laughing. Oh my God, the audience is laughing! I step closer to the stage – a big don't in the theatre because if I can see the audience, they can see me – but I have to look. I see an edge of the seating area. Yup, the kids are cracking up. I can see three adults. One is nodding, one is smiling and one is frowning. Okay. Not bad.

Eddie North as Joey starts his spoken/Seuss-rapped section and the audience starts clapping in time with his rhythm.

When the adults sing: "They're not people to us, they're a fail or a pass, it's better to think that than get close and attached," and the last note trails off, the students in the audience immediately start clapping and yelling, someone shouting "Awesome!" I think our noble ending message that maybe there's a reason for teachers not getting too close to students is lost in the moment, but at least people are cheering.

```
(Exit all except Cop-sical, Class-sical
and Doc-sical.)
```

SCENE 2: OUTSIDE DOMINION HIGH SCHOOL, IMMEDIATELY AFTERWARD

```
COP-SICAL

Someone's gonna get in BIIIIGGG trouble
for that graffiti on the side of the
school. Any idea who did it?
```

CLASS-SICAL

No, but man is the Prin-sical mad! Graffiti on her school, AND it says she sucks. So she's twice as mad.

DOC-SICAL

That kid Joey is always doing graffiti.

COP-SICAL

Is he a bad kid? Would he do something like this?

CLASS-SICAL

He's lazy and shiftless. He doesn't apply himself in class and he's always doodling.

COP-SICAL

Sounds like a real suspect.

(Music starts. ENSEMBLE wanders onstage.)

Patrick nails the new beginning of "Biggest Blame Fool", making me thank the theatre gods again, and Tom, for bringing him to us. Editing the *Seussical* soundtrack CD to fit our abbreviated version of the score would have taken more time than we had. With Patrick, we just said, "start here" and he made it work.

Jocelyn, I admit, does a good job spewing snide cynicism at Morton as the song picks up pace. Our dance interlude is weak, another victim of our lack of time, but we whirl around the stage criss-crossing and linking arms for a while before returning to the song.

When Emily comes on as Prin-sical and belts out "What the heck do my eyes see?" like the R-E-S-P-E-C-K line in the original show, I literally feel my eyes bulge in surprise. Where did that come from? It was like she was channeling Aretha. The second-to-longest song in the show goes on and on, and I'm loving it. We rock the lines and the singing and the story-telling. At the end, everyone wanders off, the adults laughing at Morton.

Alex and I stop in the wings and wait to go back on. Since no one is paying any attention to us, he sneaks a kiss on the cheek as the lights come up on "Joey" at his desk in his bedroom. "After you, Mom-sical," he whispers, making me smile. Finally. Alex and me, acting together, with an audience.

We walk onstage for our moment in the spotlight.

SCENE 3: JOEY'S BEDROOM, SAME AFTERNOON

POP-SICAL

Joey, we've told you before
Maybe a hundred times
Not so much computer
You're bound to go blind

You sit and you play
All that video stuff
Put it away now
Enough is enough!

JOEY

But it's not just for fun.
I'm making something new
I'm creating a vision
That's what I wanna do

With the rest of my life
This is my career
I'm gonna make video games
The people will cheer!

MOM-SICAL

Nice try, little Joey
But you need to do more
Then sit around clicking
You're becoming a bore.

JOEY

But all last weekend
I didn't play games
Or make any videos
I don't deserve blame

MOM-SICAL

But that was because
We took your PC
And instead all you did
Was think, eat and sleep

You stared out that window
Looking at the yard
And dreaming your dreams
Why is it so hard

To be like a normal boy
Who runs and who plays
Doing normal boy things
All through the day?

JOEY

But--

POP-SICAL

No buts now son.
We've made a decision
Its Military School for you
Where you'll learn some precision

They'll train you to act
But not think so much
And none of that dreaming

```
Or imaginary stuff.

              MOM-SICAL

(More tenderly)
I know how this feels, Joey,
But we heard from the school
They say you're in trouble
You have broken the rules

So just go quietly
Whether you're ready or not
And who knows - this new school
You might like it a lot.

(MOM-SICAL AND POP-SICAL exit.)
```

While Eddie as Joey breaks into "It's Happening", based on "It's Possible", I look for Adrienne, finally finding her in the hallway behind the stage.

"Yale, Yale, Yale, Yale," I chant, coming up behind her and giving her a giant hug.

She turns, unable to suppress her smile.

"I didn't screw it up too much?"

"Adrienne, you were awesome! I think you should come to Yale School of Drama with me."

"Yeah, right," she scoffs, but she's beaming.

"Come on, let's go watch. The first boob song is coming up."

We bounce back to the wing to watch.

*A*fter Eddie kicks ass with his solo, Lucey as Mildred starts her *pièce de résistance*, "The World's Smallest Boobs on Miss Mildred McBuff". I have no idea if Principal Zowicki is fuming at our interpretation of "The One Feather Tail of Miss Gertrude McFuzz", but the audience starts howling when Lucey gets to her line "how flat is my chest?" and they don't stop for the rest of the short song. Lucey's chest is hidden under a baggy, shapeless tunic but everyone at Crudup knows what's under there. Maybe Alex should have asked the audience to suspend disbelief in his introductory remarks.

As soon as Mildred finishes her lament, the music changes to a bouncing, vampy tune as Kristina as In-Betweenzy sashays on, launching right into "Miss Big Bazooka", which is based on "Amayzing Mayzie". No Bird Girl back-up singers in the Senior Class Play due to lack of birds.

A twinge of regret that I'm not playing Mayzie's alter ego crosses my heart, but I banish it by thinking of Alex and how we're getting to play off each other as Mom-sical and Pop-sical.

Kristina and Lucey are hysterical in their back and forth. Cast members around me, and the audience, are cracking up. When my chest spazzes, I look at it guiltily and realize I'm laughing at Lucey's performance, too. She is very funny. So what, I let myself off the hook. It's senior year. This is our play. Old grudges have no place here, at least for the length of this song. I laugh out loud and smile at Foster and Alex standing next to me.

Miss Big Bazooka...In-Betweenzy, Mildred
```
     (based on "Amayzing Mayzie")

             IN-BETWEENZY

    (Spoken)
    POOR LITTLE MILDRED,
    A SAD, SAD SIGHT
    I'M GONNA TAKE PITY
    AND SHOW YOU THE ROPES
    AND THEN BABY, YOU'LL BE ALL RIGHT!

    (Singing)
    I WAS ONCE A PLAIN UGLY FREAK
    LIKE YOU ARE
    CHEST SO FLAT
    I SWEAR I'D BEEN CURSED AT BIRTH
    BUT YOU CLEARLY OUT-DO ME,
    LAMEST GIRL ON THE EARTH
    WHEN IT COMES TO CLEAVAGE
    YOU'RE CLEARLY THE WORST

                MILDRED

    THANKS, IN-BETWEENZY
```

                    IN-BETWEENZY

THEN I BEGGED MY MOM
FOR SOME PLASTIC SURGERY
NEEDED BOOBS WITH SOME OOMPH
NOT JUST ONE BUT TWO
WANTED SOMETHING FANTASTIC,
BARBIE PLASTIC WOULD DO
THE DAY CAME,
SAW MY SILICONE DREAMS COMING TRUE

NOW I'M...
MISS BIG BAZOOKA
BOMBASTIC AND PLASTIC IS ME NOW
MISS BIG BAZOOKA

                       MILDRED

THEY'RE SO ROUND AND TIGHT

                    IN-BETWEENZY

MISS BIG BAZOOKA
THE BOYS ARE ALL DROOLING AT ME NOW
MISS BIG BAZOOKA
THIS HAS CHANGED MY LIFE!

LEFT OR RIGHT

                       MILDRED

GEE, THEY'RE MARVELOUS

                    IN-BETWEENZY

FIRM FOR LIFE

                       MILDRED

I'M SO ENVIOUS

                    IN-BETWEENZY

KEEP 'EM HIGH
I LOVE MY MARVELOUS BOOBS

<pre>
                    MILDRED

    I REALLY WANT SOME LIKE THOSE

                  IN-BETWEENZY

    ROUND AND ROUND

                    MILDRED

    LIKE I'VE NEVER SEEN

                  IN-BETWEENZY

    UP AND DOWN
    HEY, YOU'RE GETTING GREEN

                    MILDRED

    THYE'RE SO COOL, I WANT SOME
    MARVELOUS BOOBS!

                  IN-BETWEENZY

    CALL THIS MAN,
    HE'LL MAKE YOU A PLAN
    HE'LL GET YOU BOOBS LIKE ME
    THEN YOU, CAN BE AS MARVELOUS
    (WELL ALMOST)
    AS SIMPLY MAR-VEL-OUS AS ME!

  (IN-BETWEENZY scribbles something on a
  business card and hands it to MILDRED.)

  Tell him In-Betweenzy sent you.

  (Exit IN-BETWEENZY and MILDRED.)
</pre>

"Look out!" Lucey whisper yells as she plows into the cast members in the stage right wing after the scene ends. "This is my quick change!"

On cue, Jocelyn and Emily appear with a colorful, low-cut shirt and a pile of bright, noisy bracelets, which they slide onto

Lucey as soon as she rips off her gray shirt-like clothing thing. Lucey adjusts her breasts with her hands for maximum cleavage, yanks out her hair elastic, flips over and musses her hair, and whips back up.

"Am I big enough?" she whispers. Lindsay and Sam don't even try to smother their laughs, making Lucey roll her eyes. "My hair, Jos – is it big enough? Never mind. Gotta go," she harrumphs, every inch the diva, and follows Sam/Morton back onto stage.

After a quick exchange in which Mildred realizes Morton could care less about her glitzy new look and enhanced body parts, Lucey exits the stage again while In-Betweenzy dumps her puppy on Morton (our version of Mayzie dumping her egg on Horton).

Soon it's time for the ensemble to glide onstage for "A Place For Me" based on "Solla Sollew".

After that, it's right on to military school.

CHAPTER 17: IT'S A HIT

SCENE 6: MILITARY SCHOOL, A WEEK LATER

(Enter GENERAL SHARK-SICAL and 2-3 military school students including JOEY, holding sticks of wood like rifles. They begin drilling.)

GEN. SHARK-SICAL

Hup, two, three, four.
Lift, two, three, four.

HALT!!!
You, why can't you get this right?
Are you blind, with no sight?

JOEY

Um, no.

GEN. SHARK-SICAL

No, what?! What's that you said?

JOEY

No, sir!

GEN. SHARK-SICAL

Well, that's better
Start using your head
Respect your leader

And do what I say
That makes it much easier
To get through the day

And follow directions
Get these, then there's more
You've got to be ready
When the day comes for war

(Kids snicker.)

What-- you don't think this affects you?
Afghanistan and Iraq
Are not going anywhere
We're still under attack

By jihadists and commies
They lurk everywhere
We must get ourselves ready
We must be prepared!

                    JOEY

(Quietly.) This is bull, that's what I
think.

                GEN. SHARK-SICAL

You must speak more clear

                    JOEY

I said, this is bull
And I'm outta here.

(Drops his "rifle" and turns to leave.)

                GEN. SHARK-SICAL

You can't leave. You'll be court-
martialed.

                    JOEY

Dude, this isn't the army

```
It's just a dumb school
And you don't control me

I don't want a life
Filled with anger and hate
If you wanted to change me
You're ten years too late.

(Exit ALL.)
```

I'm so excited for the final few scenes, and so sad it's almost over. This is the best show Alex and I have ever done together. I'm dying to hold his hand, or even stand next to him, but there are too many people around. I walk behind the ancient scrim to the other wing, breaking a CDC rule, instead of using the hallway behind the stage like I should. Now I can see Alex across the stage but can't be tempted to reach out to him.

SCENE 7: DOMINION, A FEW DAYS LATER

```
(Enter MORTON, followed by MILDRED, her
look back to normal.)

                 MILDRED

Morton, Morton -- I figured it out! I
know who painted the graffiti!

                 MORTON

No way! Really, Mildred? Who did it?
What did you find?

                 MILDRED

Look. Look at this.

(Hands him the business card IN-
BETWEENZY gave her but they are
interrupted by CLASS-SICAL walking on.)
```

                    CLASS-SICAL

You. Morton. In the Prin-sical's office
now.

                    MORTON

Me? Why?

                    CLASS-SICAL

You're in big trouble. Let's go.

                    MILDRED

Morton -- I've got to do something. I'll
meet you there!

(Exit ALL. Lights down.)

SCENE 8: DOMINION, PRIN-SICAL'S OFFICE, SAME DAY

(Lights up on PRIN-SICAL, standing, and
2 SCHOOL COMMITTEE MEMBERS sitting at a
table. CLASS-SICAL and MORTON enter.)

**The School Comm. Vs. Morton the Foolish
One (Based on "The People Versus Horton
the Elephant")**

                    PRIN-SICAL

    MORTON, WE BROUGHT YOU HERE,
    BECAUSE THE SCHOOL COMMITTEE IS
    WORRIED

                    CLASS-SICAL

    OH YES THEY'RE WORRIED NOW!

PRIN-SICAL

THEY CALLED THIS MEETING TO LET YOU
DEFEND YOURSELF

MORTON

DEFEND, DEFEND, DEFEND MYSELF?

SCHOOL COMM. MEMBERS

DEFEND, DEFEND, DEFEND, DEFEND --
YOURSELF

PRIN-SICAL

(Spoken)
THE STUDENT IS CHARGED WITH WILLFUL
HALLUCINATION
AND STIRRING UP THE STUDENT
POPULATION

MORTON

(ignore his spoken line)

PLEASE WAIT, SIR
AND MADAM, I
DON'T KNOW WHAT YOU'RE ON ABOUT

ADULTS

WORLD'S BIGGEST FOOL
AT DOMINION HIGH SCHOOL

MORTON

YOU KNOW I
DID'NT DO THIS
WHY ARE YOU MAKING THIS STUFF UP?

ADULTS

WORLD'S BIGGEST FOOL
AT DOMINION HIGH SCHOOL

PRIN-SICAL

QUIET! QUIET! QUIET IN THIS ROOM!

LET'S HEAR FROM SOMEONE
WHO SAW THE WHOLE THING

MORTON THE FOOLISH ONE
WAS DOING WHAT AND WHEN

(tempo change)

COP-SICAL

OK
HE'S THE WORLD'S BIGGEST FOOL
IN THE ENTIRE SCHOOL
AS EVERYONE HERE CAN TELL
WORLD'S BIGGEST FOOL
JUST A CRAZY OLD FOOL
THE KIDS SAY HE DID IT,
OR HE HELPED

THAT BOY JOEY THE ONE WHO LEFT
HE MUST BE GUILTY

ADULTS

GUILTY!

COP-SICAL

GUILTY!

ADULTS

GUILTY!

CLASS-SICAL

KICK HIM OUT OF SCHOOL OH PLEASE!

SCHOOL COMM. MEMBERS

YOU'RE IN TROUBLE NOW,

```
YOU'RE IN TROUBLE NOW
YOU'RE IN TROUBLE NOW
```

                    MORTON

OBJECTION!

                    ADULTS

OVERRULED!

          SCHOOL COMM. MEMBERS

```
YOU'RE IN TROUBLE NOW,
YOU'RE IN TROUBLE NOW
YOU'RE IN TROUBLE NOW
```

                    MORTON

OBJECTION!

                    ADULTS

OVERRULED!

          SCHOOL COMM. MEMBERS

```
YOU'RE IN TROUBLE NOW,
YOU'RE IN TROUBLE NOW
YOU'RE IN TROUBLE NOW (repeat)
```

                    MORTON

STOP!!!

```
(spoken)
YOU CAN CALL ME A JERK
YOU CAN CALL ME A FOOL
I'M NOT LIKE THE OTHER KIDS
YOU DON'T THINK THAT'S COOL
I'VE DONE NOTHING WRONG HERE
THROW ME OUT OF YOUR SCHOOL
JUST BECAUSE I'M NOT LIKE YOU
AND I AM BREAKING SOME DUMB RULE
```

(sung)
US KIDS HERE
LET ME BE CLEAR
LISTEN UP AND LISTEN CLOSE
WE'RE REAL
WE'RE PEOPLE HERE
SO WHAT WE'RE YOUNG
COMPARED TO MOST

(spoken)
YOU CAN DO WHATEVER WITH ME,
PRIN-SICAL
I DON'T REALLY CARE AT ALL

(sung)
BUT PLEASE BE FAIR
'CAUSE JOOO--EEY DID NOTHING
AAAA-AT ALL

                    PRIN-SICAL

(Spoken)
BASED ON ALL THAT WE'E HEARD
IT'S PLAIN TO SEE
THAT MORTON IS INCAPABLE OF
TELLING THE TRUTH

OR WORSE YET,
HE ACTUALLY PAINTED THAT GRAFFITI
ON OUR PRECIOUS SCHOOL

SO ABOUT THAT PAINT

                    ADULTS

OOH, THAT PAINT

                    PRIN-SICAL

SO ABOUT THAT PAINT...

                    ADULTS

ABOUT THAT PAINT...

PRIN-SICAL

AND AS FOR THAT PAINT
SO YOU MUST
WASH, WASH, WASH, WASH, WASH IT
WITH YOUR OWN HANDS SO YOU CAN SEE
THAT YOU WERE WRONG

MORTON

(Spoken)
WASH IT! BUT WAIT!
IT ISN'T MY CRIME
WHAT HAVE I BEEN SAYING
ABOUT TWENTY TIMES

WAIT A MINUTE, WAIT A MINUTE
WHAT DID MILDRED SAY?
SHE GAVE ME THIS BUSINESS CARD
TO SAVE THIS GRIM DAY
SO LET ME JUST READ IT
IT SAYS "IN-BETWEENZY"
AND LOOK AT THAT WRITING
IT MATCHES THE GRAFFITI!

ADULTS

WASH, WASH, WASH, WASH, WASH IT

MORTON

ATTENTION EVERYBODY
ATTENTION RIGHT NOW
I'VE GOT SOME REAL PROOF HERE
OF A REAL CRIME SO FOUL

THAT JOEY DIDN'T DO IT
LIKE I HAVE ALWAYS SAID
IT WAS NOT HIS STYLE
BUT THE IDEA'S STUCK IN YOUR HEAD

(Cut some here, 4:00-4:18 in video)

(Hands the card to the PRIN-SICAL who
reads it and tears it up.)

ADULTS

WASH IT, WASH IT
WASH IT, WASH IT
WASH IT, WASH IT
WASH IT, WASH IT

MORTON

(Spoken)
I DON'T GET IT,
WHAT'S WRONG WITH YOU
THAT WAS ALL THE PROOF,
THERE IN FRONT OF YOU

PRIN-SICAL

(Spoken)
THIS SMALL CARD IS NO PROOF,
IT'S A CONFESSION WE NEED
THAT'S ALL I CAN LISTEN TO,
NO -- PLEASE DON'T PLEAD

ADULTS

WASH IT, WASH IT
WASH IT, WASH IT

MORTON

JUST LISTEN! (Repeat several times,
at same time as Adults)

NARRATOR

NOW FOR THIS DARK MOMENT,
OUR MORTON WAS LOST
HE HAD TO BE HEARD SOON,
AND AT ANY COST
IT WAS ALL UP TO MILDRED,
MAYBE HER PROOF
COULD CONVINCE THEM OF THE TRUTH

```
                    ADULTS

             WASH IT, WASH IT

             (MILDRED  enters,  dragging  a
             guilty-looking IN-BETWEENZY.)

                   MILDRED

         WAIT!!!!!

             (Music ends, at 5:11 in video)

         (Everyone  turns  to  them  and  freezes.
         MILDRED  pushes  IN-BETWEENZY  up  to  the
         PRIN-SICAL.  IN-BETWEENZY  reluctantly
         nods  at  the  PRIN-SICAL,  admitting
         guilt.)

                  CLASS-SICAL

         Well,  I'll  be  damned...do  you  see  that?
         It  looks  like  In-Betweenzy  is  here  to
         confess,  and  Morton  isn't  such  a  fool
         after all. He was right all along.

                  PRIN-SICAL

         This  session  of  the  School  Committee  is
         adjourned.

         (All exit except MORTON and MILDRED.)
```

The audience laughs when they should throughout the song, which is a good sign, and cheers at the end of the scene when Morton and Joey are proven not guilty.

Mildred and Morton have a short touching talk and walk off hand-in-hand.

Eddie as Joey takes his seat at his bedroom desk. Alex and I walk on to wrap up the show.

```
              POP-SICAL

 Joey, we're happy
 To have you at home

                JOEY

 I'd rather be here, Pop,
 Then live on my own

 I can't do the army
 I don't think like them
 And I need to make art please
 So let me stay home

              MOM-SICAL

 Of course you can stay, son
 Your name has been cleared
 We always believed you
 We love you, my dear.

 (They hug.)

 (Curtains close. END OF PLAY)
```

"We're terrible parents," Alex laughed as we jogged off stage and got ready for bows.

"I know, right? First, we don't listen to our own son and send him off to military school because maybe he vandalized the school. Then when he's proven innocent, we say we knew it all along. We suck!" Alex and I cracked up. For a second, I wondered what our kids would look like if we had them some day.

Then I was swept up in the rush of our small sea of seniors flooding back onstage for curtain call. Bows were pretty informal. We all stood in a line and stepped forward one by one while the audience yelled and whistled.

I felt as satisfied as I did after any full-length play I'd been in. Our one-act play was a success – funny and, hopefully, delivering a message. Alex and I got to act together. I wrote a kick-ass script, and he directed. What more could a girl want?

Alex and I were getting ready to separate in the hallway when kids started streaming into the backstage area from the school lobby.

"Hey," an adult voice said as a firm hand gripped my arm. My stomach dropped a foot. Principal Zowicki? Fishbein?

"Amazing job, you two." I turned to see Ms. English releasing my arm. I hadn't realized she was back already. "That's when you say 'thank you'," she said in response to our stares.

"Thanks," Alex and I said in unison.

"Really, great job. Now I see what you were talking about. You guys are pretty good at creating your own shows. It was funny and biting satire. A perfect first Senior Class Play." She beamed at us, her blonde hair reflecting the glow of the fluorescent hallway lighting.

"You don't think– Do you know if any of the other teachers are mad?" I asked, breaking my dad's rule of not asking a question if you don't want to hear the answer.

"Please. If they are, they need to get thicker skins. Kids have been making fun of teachers since the beginning of time. Being made fun of is part of our job description." She was one-hundred percent serious. Sweet. "I'm going to go congratulate the others. See you at rehearsal on Monday." And she swept herself down the hallway, leaving me and Alex with slow smiles spreading across our faces.

"Oh, yeahhh," he dragged out, raising his hand for a high five. "Our deed is done."

CHAPTER 18: PERSPECTIVE

Alex and I resumed our regularly scheduled roles at home pretty much right after the play ended that night.

My parents insisted on driving us both home, even though Alex said he could find another ride. So he and I sat in the back seat of Dad's car like old times. I played with the pile of rubber and string bracelets on my wrist rather than look at Alex. Mom, the bloodhound, kept turning around to look at us.

"It's nice to see you two getting along better," she said, but the way she said "nice" made it sound like she thought the exact opposite. "You did a good job working onstage together."

I froze for a second.

"Plays bring out the best in people, I guess," Alex offered, not looking at me. "I mean, you have to work together."

"Well, some people. Shows bring out the diva in other people," I said, not even trying to be annoying but apparently succeeding anyway.

"Whatever," Alex said.

"I wasn't talking about you, Alex. You don't need to get pissy."

"Okay, never mind," Mom sighed, turning back around.

DO YOU THINK SHE BOUGHT IT? Alex texted me when we'd retreated to our bedrooms at home.

I THINK SO BECAUSE SHE LET US UPSTAIRS ALONE FOR ONCE, I answered. My parents were having a cocktail in front of the living room fire.

LET'S ADD ANOTHER SCENE TO BE SAFE, he texted, and before I could wonder what he meant, he knocked at my door.

"Do you think you could turn down your music? I have to study," he yelled through the closed door.

I threw the door open, slipping right into character. "It's not that loud. What's your issue? Put on your headphones if you don't want to hear it."

"If I wanted to hear my own music, I would use headphones, but I'm trying to *study*. I need it quiet for that."

"Oh, well excuse me, I guess you're used to being the only kid in your house." Oops, that was too close to a sensitive spot since his older brother had been been hauled off to jail for dealing drugs or something.

"You know what? I wish I'd gone to California after all." He looked mad but I couldn't tell if he was acting. He stomped into Jesse's room and slammed the door.

I channeled all my fake anger into the words "Me too" and slammed my door.

I couldn't even smile at our strong performances. I grabbed my cell.

SADIE: SORRY ABOUT THE BROTHER COMMENT.

ALEX: ??? THAT WAS A GOOD SCENE WASN'T IT?

SADIE: SO YOU DON'T REALLY WISH YOU'D GONE TO CA?

ALEX: OF COURSE NOT. NIGHT.

SADIE: NIGHT.

A week later, the only lingering reminder of our successful Senior Class Play was the *Seussical* cast messing up our lyrics in rehearsal because we still had *Whoosical* lyrics on the brain.

Weirdly, I didn't cry when *Whoosical* ended, like I did after every other show I'd ever been in, I think because we jumped right back into *Seussical* rehearsals, and I didn't have to say good-bye to my *Whoosical* cast mates.

But that didn't stop a little post-show letdown from slipping in. Why couldn't we bottle the high of a performance and take sips over the following weeks to spread the good feeling around and make it last longer?

*M*aybe she was toying with us, but Ms. English seemed more open to our *Seussical* suggestions after seeing the Senior Class Play. She actually asked for our input before deciding to cut "The Circus McGurkus" from the show. I agreed we didn't have the time or, I hate to say it, talent to pull off the extravagant number. Lucey was pissed because she wanted to play acrobat and perform her signature back handspring which, according to rumor, she did at every basketball game anyway, as part of the cheerleading routines.

Definitely, most of us in the cast felt new respect for Ms. English, because of her positive reaction to *Whossical*. And she actually made a few comments about the weak spots in our senior play – one pacing and one dialogue – that I completely agreed with. It felt weirdly good to be on the same page as her.

Other than her, the teachers we expected to laugh about *Whossical* did, and the ones we expected to hate the show did. The ones we didn't think would bother to go didn't. Most important, Principal Zowicki didn't seem to care what we'd done, although my dad said at dinner one night that she was appointing a teacher advisor for next year's Senior Class Play. School Committee member Fishbein hadn't even seen the show. Guess she was only a theatre freak when her daughter Ada was onstage. So our play was a success with the other students and we weren't getting in trouble for crossing any lines. Perfect.

Seussical rehearsals entered the fun stage, when we were far enough into it that we could run entire scenes at a time, with flub-ups and ad libs giving us lots of reasons to laugh despite working hard. English was becoming a pretty good director and Fishbein's main job was running us through the songs. Since we weren't choosing new songs and writing new lyrics like for last year's show, there was nothing for her to complain about except when someone forgot their line or their note.

Or so I thought. Then she threatened to kick Lindsay out of the show if he missed one more rehearsal.

"I don't get it. We're only a few weeks away from opening. Why does she want to screw things up now?" Kristina asked backstage.

"Your mother's the choreographer. Why don't you ask her what's going on?" Foster pointed out.

Kristina shrugged. Her mother was a pushover, we all knew it, bowing to whatever Fishbein said. No way she was going to divulge intel, even if she had any. Mrs. Kent's weakness actually made me appreciate my mother's usually annoying stiff backbone.

"Fishbein's been in a bad mood, legit, since the beginning of rehearsals this year," Ben said.

"We know why," I said. Foster's brow wrinkled as he waited for my explanation. "She's been in a bad mood ever since the *casting*. Because little Ada didn't get a good role."

"Ohhhh," they all said, nodding.

"Hey, it could be worse," Foster said. "At least Ada's Thing 1 not Thing 2. That's top billing, sort of." We laughed. Ada wasn't so bad, but anything that upset her mother I was cool with.

"So, do you think she wants to slide Ada into Lindsay's role? Could she do Cat in the Hat and pull it off?" Kristina asked.

I nodded again. "I think she could. But that wouldn't be fair. Lindsay's a senior and he won the role fair and square. Although it is annoying that he's never here and he doesn't know his lines yet." My friend and thespian loyalties collided.

Ms. English yelled from the auditorium. "Everyone onstage, please."

"Just to be safe, I'm going to warn Lindsay to get his act together," Tom said as we strolled toward the stage.

"Nice pun, Tom," I said, nudging him with my elbow.

"Huh?" he said, making me laugh. Tom and Adrienne were both sharp in their own ways, but when it came to theatre references, they were useless.

"Let's run 'Biggest Blame Fool' again," Ms. English said when we were all gathered. "And again. And again. 'Til we get it right."

We groaned but happily. I liked this number because it was my first real entrance in the show. I felt alive and unnaturally outgoing as I introduced Mayzie to the house in word and song, my vocal swelling on the last 'talk about me' as I did my best Ethel Merman imitation. It wasn't an easy note for me but I nailed it.

So I was surprised when Ms. English brought up those very lines in her notes at the end of rehearsal.

"Mayzie's opening lines were a little giddy, Sadie. She needs to be pushier and bossier, to set the tone for the rest of the show. After all, this is a bird who gives up her own egg."

I nodded mechanically but inside I fumed, not listening as she continued her notes.

When rehearsal broke up, Lucey bumped into me and smirked. "Nice job, Mayzie," she said sarcastically.

"What's the matter?" Adrienne asked, catching up with me and watching Lucey walk off. "What's up with her?" she asked as we walked out of the auditorium together.

"Oh, who cares about Lucey. Ms. English said I was giddy. Giddy! What does that even mean? I'm not supposed to be enthusiastic onstage? It's called stage acting and it's supposed to be over the top, for crying out loud. And Mayzie is a totally over the top character." I felt myself slipping into a funk.

"Um, Sadie, what she said wasn't that bad. She was just giving comments to lots of people." I felt Adrienne studying me as we walked. "Is everything okay?" She linked her arm through mine when we hit the sidewalk. I didn't answer. "Don't worry, it will all be fine."

Sometimes, I swore being in a bad mood made more bad things happen. Like the negativity in my body from Ms. English's unhelpful comment was a magnet attracting all other negative debris in the universe.

Dinner was a royal fun-fest that night.

It all started when Alex turned down the peas Mom passed.

```
                    ALEX

No  thanks,  Mrs.  Perkins.  I  don't  like
peas. No offense.

(He passes the bowl of peas to Dad.)
```

SADIE

(Innocently.)

What do yo mean, you don't like peas?

ALEX

What I said. I don't like peas.

(ALEX sounds way more annoyed than the situation calls for. SADIE makes a mental note to talk to him about over-acting.)

SADIE

Yes, you do. We eat peas together all the time.

(MOM and DAD turn to look at Sadie.)

I mean, we used to.

(SADIE stares at ALEX but he refuses to look at her.)

Come on, Alex, remember? Sitting in your back yard, eating peas that time your mother had just got back from the grocery store. And I'm sure there were other--

ALEX

Those were raw. It's different.

SADIE

Oh, well excuse me--

                         DAD

Okay, okay. I'm starting to miss
listening to Sadie and Jesse argue at
the dinner table.

I will eat Alex's share of the peas and
the world will be fine.

(Dramatically scoops three large
spoonfuls of peas onto his plate.)

                         MOM

Let's talk about something more
interesting.

(Scans the ceiling as if looking for a
topic to pull from the air.)

How about college?

(Looks directly at SADIE.)

Alex tells me he's almost done with his
applications. And we're going to the
financial aid seminar at the school next
week.

(SADIE stares at her   mother,
dumbfounded.)

What? (Innocently.)

You didn't mention it, so I assumed you
didn't want to go. Which is short-
sighted, by the way, because it's not
like we can't use some financial aid.

(SADIE looks hurt. MOM's voice softens.)

```
Don't worry, Sadie. I'll find out what
you need to know. It makes more sense to
do it this way.
```

```
                    SADIE
```

```
Oh, sure. It makes more sense for my own
mother to go to a school event with my
ex-boyfriend since she's planning his
future not mine.
```

```
                    MOM
```

```
(Blinks, shakes her head.)
```

```
So, what is the status of your list? Any
shorter?
```

I couldn't even script this in my head anymore, it was so annoying.

"Mom," I complained, my frustration at basically everything coming through, "how can I decide which schools to apply to if we haven't visited them yet?"

"Sadie," she put her fork down, echoing my irritated voice, "I've told you, we're not going to visit thirty colleges, which at last count is what you had on your list. Have you even started narrowing down your list yet?" She took my silence as a no, correctly. "You're going to run out of time. You have to take charge of this. I can't do it for you."

"You haven't done that yet? That's unlike you, sweetie," said Dad. "I thought you were dying to get through your undergrad experience so you could conquer Yale School of Drama?" You would think the teacher in the family would be more on top of my college application process, but he always left that sort of thing to my mother. "Remember to shoot high with your choices. I have faith in you," he said, apparently trying to boost my confidence.

"Yes, but you also need some safety schools," my mother added, sounding like the school guidance counselor.

Safety schools, stretch schools, BAs, BFAs, theatre majors, musical theatre minors, conservatories, liberal arts colleges, private, public...what sounded like the world's greatest bowl of opportunity last year sounded like the world's most confusing assignment this year.

I knew why I was procrastinating on my applications. I was confused as hell. I didn't have a clue how to turn my list of thirty schools into a short list, and my mother was only letting me apply to ten schools max.

"Hey, we don't know a lot about these artsy schools, but you know who would?" Dad asked, getting all excited. "Ariana English, your new director. Doesn't she have a background in performing arts? Why don't you ask her for some advice, honey?"

The thought of asking Ms. English for help was mortifying. Why would she want to help me?

"Mom, Dad, give me a break. I'll get to it, soon. It's been a little busy lately, between *Seussical* and *Whossical* and schoolwork and Mrs. Holman being sick–"

"Oh, like you even care?" Alex said, making all the breath leave my body in one sharp gust. "When's the last time you asked about her? You don't even visit her anymore." Tears pooled in my eyes but I quickly blinked them back and focused on my plate. I couldn't talk. I was afraid my voice would break.

After an uncomfortable silence, my parents started discussing the upcoming special town meeting, sparing me and Alex from further conversation. He and I ate, or pretended to, in silence.

"*T*his situation is torture," I complained to Adrienne on the phone from my bedroom after dinner. "I can't be nice to him or my parents worry we're getting back together. I can't argue with him or they yell at us to get along. I can't ask him what's wrong and why he's being so mean to me, 'cause I'm not supposed to care. And on top of that, it really sucks when I have a bad hair day 'cause there's no avoiding him." I sobbed quietly.

"Sadie, forget about the bad hair days," Adrienne soothed. "You can't keep trying to look perfect at home. You're driving yourself crazy. Home is where we get to be slobs and not wear make-up and not brush our hair and wear crappy clothes." I cried softly in response. "Alex doesn't care what you look like. Wait, that sounded bad. He does care, he thinks you're beautiful I'm sure, like I do, but he doesn't care if sometimes you look a little less beautiful. You know that, right?"

I sniffled.

"Look at it this way. Do you care if *he* has a bad hair day? Or if he's wearing a ripped shirt?"

"Adrienne, you know it's different for boys. They just look cuter when they're scruffy. No one likes a scruffy girl." I grabbed another tissue from my bedside table.

Adrienne sighed and I felt a little badly for being such a tough subject.

"Okay, fine, I'll try not to worry about it so much," I said.

"Good. And let's get you two together at my house soon. You need to talk."

I nodded. Adrienne would take care of it.

CHAPTER 19: FINE FEATHERS

*A*lex didn't even come to the breakfast table in the morning, claiming he'd overslept and grabbing an apple on the way out. I was sure it was because of last night. On the school bus, I took a deep breath and turned to him.

"What's wrong?" I asked.

He took a huge bite of his apple. "What do you mean?" he mumbled.

"I mean, last night's dinner. Are you really mad at me about your mother? I'm sorry I don't ask about her more, but we're not together that much and I admit sometimes I forget. And I will start visiting her again, now that *Whossical*'s over. But, I–"

"Whoa, slow down. Sadie, I'm not mad. That was our little act, remember?"

"That, was an act?" I hmphed and looked away for a second. "So you're not mad about any of it? Your mother? The peas? My general existence?"

"Sadie, what the hell are you talking about? It's not like we started pretending to be broken up yesterday. We've been at this for a while." His green eyes, serious and steady, did not have their usual positive effect on me.

"Alex, you had me in tears last night at dinner! Well, almost."

"Yeah, I saw that, and you have to be more careful. You can't let your parents think you care about anything I say or do," he said, still happily crunching away.

"Aaargh, you drive me crazy, Alex Holman," I seethed.

"Wait a second. Are *you* mad?" he asked, stopping his annoying chewing.

"I'm not happy, that's for sure," I muttered, crossing my arms. We stewed for a minute.

"Well, I'm not all that happy about this, either," he finally said. "But, it's what we have to do." He pulled a book from his backpack and opened it. "I have to study for my Spanish quiz or I'm failing for sure." We rode the rest of the way in silence.

"*N*o, no, no, Sadie!" Ms. English said in the middle of rehearsal, horrifying me. "Mayzie may be a tough bird but she's not a total bitch," the teacher said, horrifying me even more. "It's like you're over-compensating. Listen, there are a bunch of ways to play this character. You've got to find the one that works best for this production, and most of all, you have to be consistent," she said.

A vise squeezed around my chest, pushing a massive lump up my esophagus. I hated my life.

"Want me to show her how to do it?" Lucey asked, all sugar and spice. "Maybe Sadie's not cut out for Mayzie. She's so wishy-washy, always changing her mind. She'd be perfect to play Charlie Brown, though." She fake smiled and scrunched up her shoulders, so pleased with herself.

Ms. English ignored her. "Listen," she said in a softer voice. "Why don't you stay after rehearsal and we'll talk about your character? I know you can do this."

Tears of anger blurred my vision. Of course I could do this. I was the most experienced actor in our cast. Or at least the most dedicated.

"Okay," I said. "Or not," I muttered, turning away.

Thankfully, she moved on to the next scene, sparing me further humiliation.

Soon after, I was called into the "costume room" – a.k.a. the Art room – to be prodded and poked by Mrs. Madison, Ben's mother, who had volunteered to be Costume Coordinator. Jocelyn's mother had signed up to help, too, but quickly resigned when she realized they were sewing costumes, not buying them.

I liked the red and hot pink feathery costume pieces Mrs. Madison showed me, which lifted my mood some, but by the time I'd been stuck with three pins, one of them actually drawing blood, my foul mood was back. I snuck away home at the end of rehearsal.

$\mathcal{B}$y the next rehearsal, I regretted that decision. I'd had no luck testing different approaches for Mayzie in my bedroom the night before, partly because I kept getting distracted by Alex making boy noises in his bedroom and the bathroom.

The world's most awkward exchange hadn't helped.

I had quietly left my room to go pee and almost bumped into Alex shutting the bathroom door.

"I wouldn't go in there, if I were you," he said, in a lame, sinister voice.

I made a scoffing noise. "Why, have I used up my minutes for today?" I asked, wondering why it was so easy to act out our roles even when my parents probably weren't listening.

"No really– Fine, never mind." Was he blushing as he stormed away?

I opened the door and stepped back as if physically pushed by the horrid smell.

"Ugh!" I said out loud, immediately wishing I could take it back. The situation was bad enough without me making Alex feel worse.

"Told you," I thought I heard him say from behind the bedroom door.

Turning as red as he probably was, I slunk back to my bedroom to wait for the malodorous fog to dissipate.

Back to Mayzie, so my unfocused work on my character hadn't produced much. The more I tried to develop the irresponsible bird, the more confused I got. I'd never had this problem before. Of course, Mayzie was my most complex character ever.

I regretted not taking Ms. English up on her offer, and decided to ask for her help after today's rehearsal.

We didn't work on any of my big scenes, so rehearsal was uneventful, relatively productive. Ben was doing an amazing job as Horton. Finally, we'd found the perfect role for a nerdy, nervous boy with an awesome voice. He and Emily, as Gertrude, played off each other so well it was crazy. It made me feel warm inside just watching them interact.

But then that made me feel crappy, because Alex and I may have felt that way about each other, but were being forced to continue our charade. It didn't help that all the girls gabbed nonstop about their dresses for the Homecoming Dance. Full-length or short? Glitzy or subtle and classical? Pastels or vibrant colors, and solid or patterned? One day, Adrienne was coy about her afternoon plans and I realized she was going dress shopping and didn't want me to feel badly so she hadn't told me.

My intense desire for Mrs. Holman to get better fast wasn't just for her sake anymore. It was for the sake of my relationship with Alex. I didn't know how much more of the act I could handle. The Homecoming Dance made everything worse. I couldn't go with my boyfriend. I couldn't even go with my friends and then have one dance with him. And it was the last Homecoming Dance of my high school career. The unfairness of it all stung.

Nails bit into my shoulder as Mrs. Madison hissed into my ear to come with her for another fitting.

"But I'm in the next scene," I whispered.

"That's okay, Ms. English won't care," she whispered back.

I wasn't so sure about that. I wasn't exactly on the good list with English right now. I looked at the director for permission to go but she was deep in discussion with Ben and Emily. Mrs. Madison was practically pulling me off balance. I sighed and followed her to the Art room.

My costume was beautiful, I had to say. The long feather tail was finally attached to my sparkly pink leotard with the super short skirt. As the most flamboyant of the birds, I got the most elaborate tail. Red fishnet stockings showed off my long slender legs. My average chest even looked okay in the halter top leotard, and the fingerless, long sheer red gloves were a nice touch.

"More feathers. You need more feathers," Mrs. Madison said through the pins between her lips. "Something for your hair, and something around the hem of this skirt, I think." She pushed and pulled me into different directions, occasionally stopping to scribble something down on a piece of paper.

"Okay, you're all set. Change and send the Bird Girls in, would you?" she asked. But when I got back to the stage, I didn't have a chance to tell Lucey, Jocelyn and Aimee to head into the Art room. I was too busy being reamed out by the director.

"Where have you been? You missed your cue," she said, sounding angrier than I'd ever heard her. "Let's have some more professionalism around her, everyone, please! We've heading into the homestretch. I need everyone here, all the time."

Despite the totally unfair attack, I decided, for the sake of the show, to humble myself and still ask for Ms. English's advice at the end of rehearsal. Professionalism she wanted? Professionalism she would get.

But when I approached her, she was surrounded by five or six parent volunteers, all asking questions.

"Let's go into the music room and sit down and talk there," she said above their chatter.

"Ms. English? Can I talk to you for a second?" I asked, as the parents moved away.

Ms. English sighed. "About what, Sadie?"

"About Mayzie. Can I get your input?" I tried to look sincere, hopeful and contrite all at the same time.

She winced. "Oh. Since you blew me off yesterday? Sorry, Sadie, but I've got a room full of parents waiting for me. Maybe some other time."

CHAPTER 20: WORDS FAIL

When Alex grabbed my hand on the bus and gave it a squeeze, in hindsight I should have squeezed back.

"Everything okay?" he asked my limp hand.

"Um, yeah. Any updates on your mother?" I asked, knowing the answer because if there had been, it would have been broadcast through my house last night or this morning.

"No, the specialist is still trying to figure out what will work. She says some days she'd rather not be cured if it means spitting in a cup one more time. At least they're injecting the drugs now so she doesn't have to choke down twenty pills every day." He sighed. "You wouldn't think it would be so hard to find a medicine that works. Maybe I should become a doctor someday so some other guy like me doesn't have to go through this when his mother gets TB."

A tear escaped my eye.

"Sadie, what's wrong? Don't worry, I'm sure they'll figure it out and she'll be fine. I didn't mean to scare you."

"That's not why I'm crying." I dabbed at my eye with the cuff of my fleece. "I'm sorry to be so selfish but I'm thinking about the Homecoming Dance tomorrow night. This is our last one, Alex! Our last chance to go as boyfriend and girlfriend. And our only chance, ever. And we can't do it. I don't even want to go if I can't go with you."

He bit his lip. "We could go separately. Maybe we'd even get voted Homecoming king and queen. That would be pretty funny, don't you think? Forced to get along for at least one song?" He gave a short, weak laugh.

"That's not funny at all. It sucks. This all sucks." I sounded like a whiny kid but this was my only time in the entire day to be myself and that's how I felt.

"What? What else sucks?" He turned to face me, the bus seat groaning.

"This," I said, waving my hand around to indicate the entire bus. "Our fourteen minutes a day of real life. Except it doesn't even feel like real life anymore. We spend twenty-three hours and forty-six minutes a day pretending we don't like each other. That's starting to feel like real life and it's wearing me down."

"It's not that bad," he coaxed. "It's more like fifteen hours, 'cause I'm not pretending when I'm asleep. In fact, I have a lot of good dreams about you, and we're never broken up in those." His megawatt smile was ineffective on me for the first time ever.

"Alex, joking is not helping."

He sighed and looked away. "I know it sucks, Sade, but can we try to keep it in perspective? I mean, my mom's been in the hospital for months – *months* – fighting a deadly disease. Pretending we're broken up so that I can stay here and still visit with her doesn't seem like such a big price to pay."

"I know, I know. You're right. I sound horrible when you put it that way." I waited for him to say I wasn't horrible. Silence. More silence. I tried to swallow the huge lump in my throat. It didn't work. Finally, he spoke.

"If it's really that hard for you, maybe we should stop."

"Stop what? Pretending to be broken up?" I asked hopefully.

"Sadie! You know I can't!" His eyes flashed and his voice amped up. "We can't have your parents throw me out because we're dating and me have to live in a foster home or with my aunt in California or whatever. I have to be able to keep an eye on my mother. Man, why is that so hard for you to understand?"

"I'm sorry. I do understand." I forced an apologetic smile. "I knew what you meant. And you're right. Maybe we should stop. Us. That's what you meant, isn't it."

"Yeah, that's what I meant. But I don't want to stop. This stupid ride may be all we get together but I'd rather have that than nothing. But if it's so hard on you, then we can stop. I can drive my mother's car to school and you won't even have to see me at all." His voice cracked and my heart broke.

But I had to admit, sometimes it felt like our bus rides made the whole situation harder, not easier. It was just a cruel tease. Not having to keep a relationship going on fourteen minutes of quality time a day sounded, in a weird way, like freedom.

"I just don't know how long I can keep acting this act," I said quietly as the bus screeched to a halt in front of the school.

"Then let me make it easy for you. You don't have to. 'Cause I can't do this alone. Let me put it in words you understand. I can't handle a one-man play, without you as my co-star. I'm not good enough to carry this show on my own."

He stood up, slung his backpack over his shoulder and practically ran off the bus.

"Mom, what is the big deal anyway?" I asked, trying to sound casual. We had just finished an Alex-less meal – he'd gone to Tom's for dinner – and Mom and I were loading the dishwasher. All day, I'd felt helpless about the Alex situation. And I really, really wanted to go to the dance with him. So I'd decided to try to reason with my parents.

"About what, honey?" Mom said, scraping sauce off a plate into the trash.

"About Alex and me. I mean, if we were still a we. People my age have boy-girl sleepovers all the time, so what would the big deal be if we were dating and he lived here for a while?"

She faced me, dirty plate mid-air. "Why the sudden interest?"

Having scripted this one in my head earlier, I was prepared. "No sudden interest. It's just that some of my friends were asking me today, and it got me wondering. I mean, don't you trust us?"

She stacked the plate in the dishwasher, stood up, rinsed her hands under the faucet, and dried them with a dish towel before turning to me. She leaned back against the sink. "I do trust you, Sadie. And I trust Alex. I trust you to be as responsible and mature as your age allows."

I put a glass on the top rack. "Sooo, you *don't* trust us. Are you really that afraid we'll jump into bed together? Come on, Mom, give us some credit."

She cleared her throat. "Let me put it this way. I don't trust the *situation*. And the way I look at it, why put you in a situation where you're likely to fail? And risk you ending up in a new situation that would change your life, not for the better?"

I scoffed. "You mean getting pregnant. Mom, I'm not Lucey Landau. I have no intention of getting pregnant until I'm ready, which won't be for years." I loaded another glass.

"Are you– were you and Alex having sex? Because you know how many times I've warned you about safe sex. You have to take precautions, whether you ask me for help or go to a clinic, and the pill doesn't protect against–"

"No! Mom! Stop. No. We didn't."

"Do you think he wanted to?"

I was losing control of the conversation. I hadn't scripted this.

There were no more dirty glasses so I re-arranged the ones I'd already loaded in the dishwasher. "Mom, this is so awkward. Can you forget I said anything?"

"No, I'm making a point. I bet he would have if you wanted to. Am I right? And that doesn't make Alex bad, Sadie. It just makes him a typical seventeen-year-old boy. But some things are just not worth the risk. That's why your father and I would not be comfortable with Alex staying here, across the hall from you and down the hallway from us, I might add, if you two were still dating."

Flight was not an option. I would have to fight. "I still don't get it. It seems to me like you just don't trust us." I bit my lip and stared into the dishwasher.

"Sadie." Her voice turned hard, making me stiffen. Uh oh. "Shit happens. Do you think *any* teenage girl wants to get pregnant? Well, okay, maybe a few do, but most don't. Accidents happen, all the time." She sighed and crossed her arms over her chest. "It happened to your Aunt Karen, you know, her sophomore year."

I looked up, against my will.

"It did?"

"Yes, it did, and it almost killed her." Mom's voice cracked, all hardness gone.

"Mom, you're being dramatic now. It's not the nineteen-fifties. People bounce back from unwanted pregnancies."

"I'm being literal. She had an abortion, secretly because she knew our parents wouldn't have allowed that, and the aftermath of emotions was too much for her. She got depressed, clinically, and dropped out of school. I was the only one she would talk to, which was too much pressure for me to handle. But this story isn't about me. When I thought she was getting suicidal, I broke down and told Gram what was going on. It was not a good phase of our lives," she said in classic Mom understatement. Then I noticed the silent tear sneaking down her cheek.

"Oh my God, Mom, it's okay." I moved around the open dishwasher and hugged her as tightly as I could. "It's okay. Aunt Karen turned out fine, didn't she."

"I know, I know, I'm sorry. I haven't talked about this in ages and it just brought it all back." She pulled back from my embrace to look me in the eye. "I'm okay. But Sadie, now you understand why I won't – why I *can't* – do anything that would increase the chances of something *unplanned* happening to you. It's not worth the risk."

"Okay, I get it. Forget I said anything. Really." I gave her a quick hug and closed the dishwasher. "It was just a theoretical discussion anyway."

"Good luck," Foster said as we walked off the elevator on the hospital's fifth floor. "I'll wait here," he said, plopping into a padded waiting room chair. I nodded and smiled weakly. I didn't even know what I was doing. Only that Alex had avoided me for thirty-one hours and I needed to know if we were actually broken up. And then, if we weren't, maybe we could plot a way to be together at the dance tonight. After all, we were good at plotting.

Foster had said yes in a heartbeat when I asked for a ride. I knew Alex would be the only one here visiting, because my mom was at work and my dad never visited Mrs. Holman without my mom.

As I turned the corner into Mrs. Holman's hallway, the nurse on duty nodded at me, recognizing me I guess. "You know you can't go in, right?" she said. "You can call her from outside if you want." I nodded and kept walking.

I stopped in the main hallway at a glass window that looked into a sort of mini-room between the hallway and Mrs. Holman's room. The set-up helped prevent the spread of the TB bacteria. Through another window, I could see into her room. I knew I could stand there collecting my thoughts, unnoticed, because Alex told me once how it drove his mother crazy that she couldn't see through the reflections of the two panes of glass.

I tried to focus on when and how to get Alex's attention, and what I was going to say, but was distracted by the stronger-than-usual combination of bleach and pine-scented cleaner. The floor must have been mopped a few minutes ago. Funny, it seemed dry.

I looked back into the room. Alex sat in a chair between his mother's bed and the window, holding her right hand. He was looking down and I wondered if he was asleep. She definitely was, her eyelids purplish and the skin on her face drawn and pale. How much weight had she lost since she came in here? Even her hair looked thinner, the brown and gray streaks merged into thin wisps pulled back into a loose ponytail. An IV pushed some fluid – saline or drugs or maybe even food – into her left wrist, and a bunch of monitors surrounded her, some bright and noisy, others dark and quiet.

I struggled again to script what I wanted to say, unable to come up with a good opening line and having no idea how long to make the scene. While I stewed, to my dismay, Alex started crying. My focus shifted from us and the dance to him and him alone. How could I make him feel better? What could I possibly say?

Alex was wiping his eye when Mrs. Holman's hand moved. She was waking up. He beamed a tired smile, which she matched. God, those two loved each other. Alex's alcoholic and abusive father disappeared when Alex was nine, and his older brother hadn't been heard from since going to jail a few years ago, so Alex and his mother only had each other. I looked down, not wanting to spy, but couldn't resist and looked back after a minute.

I heard their murmurs through the glass. When she pulled their interlaced hands toward her and kissed his knuckles, I saw the thin, wiry shape of her forearm muscle. He stood up, making his chair scuff, and leaned over to kiss her forehead. He straightened a few strands of her hair and sat back down, never letting go of her hand, even when he reached to pull his chair back to the bedside.

Words could not solve everything, I realized with a shock. I loved the power of words, but now I saw they could also be completely, utterly useless.

I sent mental kisses to Alex and his mother, and left.

$\mathcal{F}$riday night. Homecoming Dance. Senior year.

Despite the pleading of Adrienne and Kristina, I didn't go. I stayed home and cried all night, for Alex and for Mrs. Holman. He spent most of the night in the hospital.

There would be other dances in my life. Just not this one.

Oh well.

"$\mathcal{D}$o you want popcorn and a movie, ice cream and TV, or just a good cry and maybe – because I'm such an awesome friend in your hour of need – a foot rub?" Adrienne asked Saturday night, holding up a small bottle of Apricot Foot Scrub.

I rubbed my eyes redder. "The movie and TV options mean going into your living room, right?" Adrienne nodded. "Then let's just stay here." I leaned back against her bed and stretched my legs out on her purple-speckled rug.

"Are you broken up for real? Do you want to talk about it?" Adrienne prodded, plopping down on the floor next to me.

I heaved the world's biggest sigh. "I don't even know. I just know I couldn't do it any more. I was getting so mixed up inside. I couldn't even tell when Alex was legit mad or faking it, or really happy or faking that. I used to understand him all the time. I–" My voice trailed off and I shrugged.

"You know what I think?" Adrienne asked, waiting until I looked at her to answer her own question. "I think that as soon as Mrs. Holman gets better and comes home, and Alex moves out of your house, that you guys will be fine."

"You really think so?" I sniffed. "Because I don't know what to think anymore."

"Yes, I really think so. Sadie, Alex adores you, and you adore him. You guys are meant to be together. Like me and Tom." She tried to hold in a huge smile but it broke through anyway. Her obvious happiness pulled me an inch out of my despair.

"You and Tom? Why are you smiling like that? Oh my God, Adrienne, did something, you know, *happen* between you two? At the dance last night?" She had my full attention now. Only Adrienne's happiness could distract me from my misery.

"Oh, nothing, except that he...said it." She tried, unsuccessfully again, to keep back a smile.

"He did? He said he loved you?" I giggled and the bubbly feeling in my throat broke up some of the Alex-driven despair stuck there. Adrienne nodded. "Did you say it back?" She nodded again. I yanked myself out of my dark place, scrambled onto my knees and hugged her ferociously.

"I'm so happy for you guys, that's awesome," I said, burying my face in her shoulder.

"Oh no, I didn't make you cry again, did I?" Adrienne asked quickly.

"No, no, of course not. I'm fine. I'm just really, really happy for you two," I said, inhaling the smell of her straight brown hair. "And, your hair smells good. What shampoo are you using?" I asked, breaking away and wiping a tear before Adrienne saw it.

We looked at each other and laughed at the same time. The world's second biggest sigh drained out of my body.

"I'm so glad you invited me over, Ade. First of all, it's been way too long. And second of all, it's actually good to be out of my house. Having your boyfriend– well, you know," I finished, not wanting to re-open the Alex conversation.

"I know. So listen," Adrienne said, turning to face me and folding her legs to sit Indian style. "I have a deep, dark confession to make, and I need your help."

"Okay," I said, uncertainly.

"I've been fantasizing about helping the parents on stage crew fail. Not that they need much help. They're doing just fine on their own–"

"Whoa. Back up. You *want* them to fail? You? Adrienne, are you feeling okay?"

"I can't help it. They're driving me crazy! We need a plan. And you know I don't really want the *show* to fail. But I want *them* to. Is that bad?" I only shook my head because she clearly wasn't done. "I feel really guilty for thinking this way. But they must be stopped before they ruin the show."

Adrienne knew more about staging shows at Crudup than anyone, student or parent, so it was really annoying that Ms. English put parent volunteers in charge of what should have been Adrienne's job.

"What are you talking about? What exactly are they doing?"

"It's lots of little things. Like Mrs. Carter wants to paint the set in a realistic style because that's the style she's good at. For *Seussical*! Now you know I can't draw or paint, but I do know what look is best for the shows we do. And *Seussical* is cartoony, not realistic." Adrienne shook her head.

"Duh. I mean, has she looked at a Dr. Seuss book lately?"

"I know, right?" Adrienne leaned forward and automatically tucked her hair behind her ear before it had a chance to swing in her face. "And she doesn't know what she's doing with the props, either. She brought in this little bitty flower last rehearsal and said, 'Look, I found the perfect clover', all proud of herself. Sadie, it was like this big," she said, making a circle the size of a quarter with her thumb and forefinger. "Almost as small as a real clover."

"That's ridiculous. You won't be able to see it from five rows back," I scoffed.

"That's what I said, but she wouldn't listen to me." Adrienne hmphed.

"Damn, Mrs. Carter," I said dramatically, "something must be done about her. Can we have her, you know, taken out?" I asked, raising one eyebrow mysteriously.

"I know a guy, who knows a guy, who knows a guy who could do it," she answered, trying to match my raised eyebrow but only succeeding in looking like she had something stuck in her eye, which made me laugh and break character.

"Seriously, maybe she can be neutralized, or at least Ms. English will override her stupid decisions," I said.

"But it's not just her. Then there's Mr. Fishbein, who's helping with set construction."

"Ada's father? He seemed all right when we met him last year, remember?"

She rolled her eyes. "Yeah, nice enough, but self-appointed safety officer, too. Get this. He won't let us put the egg/nest/tree on wheels because it's not safe. He's afraid it will move when you or Ben climb on it and someone might get hurt."

"I haven't even seen it yet. Can it be carried on instead?"

"Sadie, this thing weighs about a hundred freaking pounds! We have to roll it on and off. It's the only way it will work. But it looks great, by the way, you're really going to like it."

"Oh, good," I drawled in a deep Tallulah Bankhead imitation, "because Mayzie must have an absolutely fabulous perch for the very brief time she can be bothered to take care of her own offspring."

"All two seconds of motherhood," Adrienne giggled. "Is it fun playing a narcissistic, pill-popping, completely irresponsible character? Especially after being Sandy last summer?"

"And don't forget slutty. Mayzie gets pregnant by some owl she had a three-week fling with. But she's still Dr. Seuss-bad, not like Ursula-bad or Bill Sykes-bad. I kind of love her."

I toyed with the idea of asking Adrienne's advice on how to play Mayzie, but character interpretation wasn't her strong suit.

We fantasized about ways to do away with the mother volunteers for a while longer, which helped me not think about Alex. Theatre was, as always, my haven.

CHAPTER 21: FIND YOUR CHARACTER

"Why isn't that egg/nest/tree on wheels?" Ms. English frowned, hands on hips. For a young, pretty teacher, she was pretty intimidating when she wanted to be. Mrs. Carter and Mr. Fishbein stopped pushing the five-foot-tall set piece toward center stage and turned to look at the director along with every cast member onstage.

"Wheels would be unsafe, Ariana. We must take the children's safety into account, after all," Mrs. Fishbein answered for her husband, walking onto the stage to look down on Ms. English, who stood in the pit at the front of the stage.

"But look at it. It's huge, and heavy. The two of them can barely move it," she said, motioning to Mrs. Carter and Mr. Fishbein. "And even if they could, we can't very well have them huffing and puffing and groaning while they push and pull it on and off stage, can we? Plus, it just takes too long. No, this won't do. We need wheels."

I looked back in the wings at Adrienne, who was grinning ear to ear.

"But Ariana–" Fishbein persevered.

"And what about the safety of our dedicated volunteers? Why, one of you could get a hernia doing this." Ms. English shook her head and grimaced. "Mrs. Carter, you'll have wheels put on that thing by the next rehearsal?" Mrs. Carter nodded. "Wonderful, thank you so much. Get those wheels with brakes on them if you're concerned about it rolling. Although it must weigh so much I don't know how it could roll on its own anyway. Now, let's get this behemoth into position so we can run the scene. And by the way, it really looks fantastic, Fred and Mona. You did a first-class job with it."

We all waited and watched while the parents maneuvered the egg/nest/tree into position center stage.

"Oh wait– before we get going again, Mona look at this perfect clover Adrienne found at the craft store," Ms. English said, reaching down and standing up again holding an eight-inch-wide, fuzzy pink ball on a green chopstick. "It's perfect, don't you think? Very Seuss-like," the teacher said, turning the perfectly symmetrical fuzz side to side as if admiring it from every angle.

"I already have a clover," Mrs. Carter said, deflated.

"Oh, all right. Bring yours to the next volunteer meeting and I'll have a look."

I couldn't wait for rehearsal to end so I could bolt offstage and corner Adrienne.

"What did you do? How did you do it? It's like you brainwashed her or something into doing everything you wanted."

Adrienne was still grinning. She probably hadn't stopped all rehearsal.

"You'll never believe what I did. It was daring. It was outrageous. It was unthinkable." I'd never seen Adrienne get all dramatic like this. She was definitely feeling good.

"What the hell did you do? Seriously?" I cocked my head and waited.

"Are you ready? I. Talked. To. Her." Adrienne titled her head back and forth with each word and smiled sweetly at the end.

"You talked to her? That's it? And now she's doing everything you say?" I made a phft sound. "Not likely. She's not that easy."

Adrienne looked slightly hurt. "Well, I did make a good argument. I decided I had nothing to lose by talking to her and trying to convince her why my way was better. It was actually pretty easy. She said she and I share the same vision for the production." I could tell Adrienne was thrilled to be taken seriously. She should be. And she deserved it.

"That's awesome, Ade, and I am very proud of you."

I scrunched up my face and went hm.

"What?" Adrienne asked.

"I was just thinking...maybe I should try talking to her, too, about something that's been bugging me. But she doesn't like me as much as she likes you." I shook my head, vetoing my own idea.

"That's silly. She likes us all the same. Just talk to her. Wait– you're not afraid of her, are you? Sadie?"

"No, of course not. She's just a teacher, after all."

"Then let's see you talk to her. Go ahead. Right now. She's still over there, getting her stuff together." Adrienne pointed her chin toward the auditorium seats.

"I'm *not* afraid of her. Just so you know."

"Then why won't you talk to her? Oh wait– I know. You're afraid of asking for help, aren't you. It's like Alex always says. You'd rather do it wrong yourself then do it right with someone's help." Adrienne smiled smugly like she'd solved America's Greatest Unsolved Mystery. "Lame-o, I'm just saying," she sang while picking up her things to go.

She turned back to me, saw me rooted in the same spot, and sighed. "Come on, let's go. And remember, Sadie, even the best actors and directors in the world have people helping them. There's nothing wrong with asking for help or ideas from someone else." She walked toward the exit.

"Of course not," I said, making that don't-be-ridiculous-of-course-I-know-that face, which was lost on Adrienne since I was behind her. I picked up my backpack and jogged to catch up with her. "That is, if you need to."

"*H*ey, snotty Sadie," Foster said cheerfully, his smile quickly fading when he noticed my look of horror. "Sorry, I meant snotty Mayzie, but it didn't sound as good. I like alliteration, you know." He wrapped his arm around my shoulders and squeezed, almost knocking me off balance as we trudged to Anatomy class. "Stop looking at me like that, you know I'm only joking," he said.

"Foster, what are you talking about?"

"Just that your Mayzie yesterday was, well, interesting." This was not good. I trusted Foster's dramatic instincts more than anyone's, except maybe my own. I rolled out from under his arm, clutched his shirtsleeve and pulled him over to a row of lockers.

"I know, my Mayzie sucks, doesn't she? Foster, help me figure out what's wrong. I've never had this problem before."

Foster swayed his shoulders back and forth a few times and made a popping sound with his lips, clearly buying time.

"You really want me to tell you what I think?" he asked.

"You know I do," I said, even though I wasn't sure I did.

"Well, it's just that your Mayzie is coming across a little schizo. I mean, in one scene she's bossy and obnoxious, and in the next she's sad and pitiful. I can't even decide if I like her or not. So, if I can't decide–"

"How is the audience going to decide," I said. My shoulders slumped.

"But you'll figure it out, Sadie, you always do," Foster said, hope lighting up his beautiful dark brown eyes.

"I don't know, Fos. This time is different. I feel so...lost."

"Don't be silly. You are not lost. You're right here. Your character may be a little lost. But you'll find her. Give it a little more time."

*D*espite Foster's attempt to be encouraging, I was more desperate than ever after our talk. I didn't have a little more time. The show was in three weeks.

I decided to take control and ask for help, two things I always thought were mutually exclusive.

Knowing she was always surrounded by parents at rehearsals, I took a page from Adrienne's script and went to Ms. English's classroom during my sixth period study hall. Luckily, she was alone, correcting papers at her desk. She raised an eyebrow in welcome.

"Hi," I said. She nodded. "Can I talk to you for a minute?" She smiled slightly.

I shifted back and forth from left to right, trying to recall the lines I'd written in my head for this scene.

"First, I should apologize for not taking your help when you offered it." Ms. English stared at me. "So, um, I'm sorry?"

"Are you asking me or telling me? I'm having trouble interpreting your inflection," she said. Man, she was not cutting me any slack.

I inhaled slowly and deeply. "I'm telling you that I am sorry about that day. Okay?"

She smiled what seemed like a genuine smile. "It's totally okay, Sadie. It was just an offer of help, not a requirement."

Huh? Back to the script.

"I was wondering if you could help me with Mayzie. I'm having a little trouble with the character. Do you have any suggestions?"

She put down her pen, stood up and walked around to the front of her desk. "Sure. Sit down and let's talk." She nodded at the first row of desks.

Since she leaned back against her desk, I sat on the closest desk instead of behind it, leaving my backpack on the floor. I planted my hands on either side of my legs and leaned forward.

"Okay, so here's the problem. I can't decide what kind of bird she really is. I mean, it seems like there are a bunch of ways to play Mayzie, and I keep switching back and forth between them without meaning to." I twisted my mouth to the side.

"I couldn't agree more. With all of that. Mayzie is probably the most complicated character in *Seussical*, and you haven't found one consistent approach to her yet. But, I know you can." She cleared some papers out of the way and scooched herself up so she was sitting on her desk, facing me.

"I assume you know about back story," she said. I nodded. "So, what is Mayzie's back story? Why is she the way she is?"

I scrunched my lips together. "I think she's just one of those birds – those girls – who thinks she's better and prettier and cooler than everyone else. And she's used to getting her own way. But I can't decide if she has a good heart inside or not."

"Is there anything in the script that tells you?"

"Not really. She maybe shows a tiny bit of regret when Horton takes better care of her egg than she does, but that's all."

"You've just answered the question. Only a tiny bit of regret. Then what?"

"Then she goes back to her carefree life, even though sometimes she complains about it."

"And that's where she ends up, isn't it? She never comes back to claim her egg."

"Right. So I guess she's a loser, after all."

"Well, wait a minute. What are the reasons someone might give up a– an egg?"

"Hmm. Either she doesn't care or she's scared. Maybe she doesn't think she can do a good job taking care of it." Ms. English circled her hand in the air, encouraging me on. "So...maybe she does care, and she's not all cold and heartless, but she'd rather give up and let someone else raise her egg than fail at it herself." Ms. English smiled sweetly. "That's it. That's it! So Mayzie isn't a horrible bird, but she's confused and scared underneath it all. She hides all that under a lot of bravado. Is that it?"

"That is definitely one interpretation that could work. So how do you convey all this in your portrayal of Mayzie?"

"Well, there needs to be some lightness and fun in her, not just attitude and bitchiness– oh, sorry." Ms. English shrugged. I continued. "So she can be vain and all, but the audience should like her, at least some of the time. I don't think anyone will like her when she gives up her own egg. But she doesn't need to be as obnoxious as I play her sometimes."

"Sounds good. And I've seen Mayzie played obnoxious and it works, but it has to be one or the other. So your Mayzie will be a flawed, somewhat sympathetic individual, yes?"

"Yes."

"I suggest you run through your lines tonight to cement this approach in your head. No more being wishy-washy, okay?" I cringed as she used the same phrase Lucey had. "Get Mayzie set in your head. Model her after someone you know if you need to. But lock her in your psyche."

"Okay, I've got it. Thanks!"

I slid off the desk, giving myself a wedgie, which I immediately picked since Ms. English was walking back to the chair behind her desk. At that precise moment, I decided to go for broke. After all, Yale School of Drama wasn't going to find me by itself.

"Um, can I ask you about something else?" I planted myself next to her desk, arms clasping my backpack to my chest for dear life.

"Sure," she said, resting a hand on the back of her chair but not sitting down. She waited, creating an appropriate dramatic pause.

"The thing is, I want to major in theatre – hopefully musical theatre – in college. And over the summer I made a killer list of schools with great theatre and musical theatre programs and degrees. But now, I don't know what to do next, and I'm running out of time and starting to freak out. A little." I opened my mouth but decided to stop there, ending with an inelegant sighing noise.

"How exactly can I help?" she asked, flicking a pencil against her tailored wool skirt.

"Well, didn't you say you majored in theatre or something? No wait – you're an English teacher so how could you have majored in–"

"Sadie," she said, interrupted my stuttering, "I majored in English literature and minored in theatre. That's what you remember me saying. And I have a lot of friends who majored in theatre, and some are making careers in the arts."

"Really?" I straightened my shoulders. "So, do you have any advice?"

"I'm not sure what you're asking me. You seem to know what you want." She flicked her straight blonde hair over her shoulder.

"But I don't. Not really. I don't understand the difference between a BA and a BFA and should I major in acting when I'm actually interested in scriptwriting too, and maybe even directing. I've been trying to research it on the Internet but there's nothing that compares the different choices. It's so confusing. Most of all, I can't tell which undergrad programs send the most people to Yale School of Drama. That's what I really want." My shoulders slumped from the sheer weight of my words.

"Oh, I see. Okay. I do remember some of this from when my friends went through it."

"Really?" I brightened again, apparently too much because she looked mildly offended.

"Really. It's not like it was that long ago, you know. I actually *do* remember applying to college, Sadie." She rolled her blue, almond-shaped eyes. I nodded, not daring to open my mouth and let something else offensive slip out. "My friend Carl got a BFA in Musical Theatre – I remember that because he was so excited. BFAs in Musical Theatre haven't been around all that long. But our friend Katie went for the BA because she wanted to take Psychology and other non-drama courses. They used to argue over which was better."

"And, which was better?"

"You know what? They're both acting regularly now and starting real careers in theatre. So I guess it doesn't matter."

"Hm. Okay," I said, wanting more information but not sure what to ask.

"I think in terms of wanting to try things besides acting, you should look at the courses required for each program. They're usually listed on the college websites, and that will tell you if you're allowed to dabble, or even concentrate, in direction, writing, et cetera, et cetera."

I stifled a giggle at her *King and I* reference, because I didn't think it was intentional.

"Oh, and there's one other thing. Not all colleges require auditions. In the world of higher arts education, that's a so-called safety school – one that doesn't make you try out. So be sure to apply to one or two of those." She must have caught the dismay in my eyes. "That's no reflection on your abilities, Sadie, it's just common sense."

I knew she was right.

"So you know what to do now?" I nodded and shrugged at the same time. "What else aren't you sure about?"

"Well, Yale. How do I know which schools will impress Yale Drama the most?"

Ms. English picked up a ruler and tapped it against her palm a few times. "Sadie, the admissions committee at Yale probably doesn't care which of the very good schools you go to. In fact, I bet if you look at the websites of the schools you're thinking about, every single one of them has at least one famous actor as an alumnus. No, Yale is going to care about what you accomplish at college, and what you show them when you apply for grad school. In the end, it's not about the school name on the diploma, it's about the talent and passion in you. It's not about what opportunities your school offers. It's about what you do with those opportunities." She thwacked the ruler against her palm.

"Now, before I get any further into inspirational poster land, let's get practical. When are your applications due?"

"A lot of them are due December first," I said.

"December first? That's next week." I nodded again. "It's a good thing Thanksgiving break starts tomorrow afternoon. Guess I know what you'll be doing over the long weekend," she said cheerfully, "when you're not working on Mayzie, that is." She smiled.

For the first time in ages, I felt like I knew what I was doing, too.

I thanked her and practically skipped out of her room, light as a feather from Mayzie's tail. Maybe I could get a mysterious stomach bug in the morning and skip the half day of school. I needed the extra time for college and Mayzie.

As I headed back to study hall, I debated modeling Mayzie on Lucey, who was also vain and bitchy and overly confident, and possibly hurting inside. But that idea appalled me for many reasons. Plus, my Mayzie would have an actual heart. That was it. Lucey with a heart. Or me with Lucey's attitude. Either way, my creation would be all Mayzie in the end. I couldn't wait for our next rehearsal.

And I couldn't wait for Thanksgiving break, either.

CHAPTER 22: OUT OF THE WOODS

*T*hanksgiving actually felt relatively normal in my house. Sad to say, it was because I barely saw Alex. He practically lived in his mom's hospital room for the holiday, totally bumming out my mom, who liked as many people as possible around the Thanksgiving dinner table. My brother Jesse came home for the long weekend. So it was back to my own family for a change.

I tried to convince myself Alex had never lived with us, and he and I had never dated, so I could focus on my life. Lying to yourself could be counted as acting, I figured, and it was kind of mandatory in this case so I could make some progress on my two non-Alex challenges: crystallizing Mayzie's character and dealing with college.

In between cooking, eating and visiting with relatives, Mom helped me make the world's biggest spreadsheet to keep track of which colleges had which degree programs, and what courses they offered and required, and whether or not they held auditions. Not to mention their location, number of students, and teacher to student ratio.

By Friday at noon, I finished Sadie's Sort of Short List of East Coast colleges, including Boston University and Emerson in Massachusetts. For stretch schools I included NYU and Carnegie Mellon, which accepted like minus two students a year in their drama programs. For "safety" schools I included Hofstra and Suffolk University because they didn't hold auditions, but as Mom kept reminding me, you still needed the grades to make the cut at those schools. Upstate New York colleges Syracuse University, SUNY-Purchase and Ithaca College all had great theatre programs, and so did Rhode Island College and UConn, which rounded out my list.

I shifted from being overwhelmed to being focused. Just reading about the different programs and looking at website photos, now that my list was manageable, made me twitch in my skin with excitement. I stopped pestering Mom about visiting schools, which I now realized had been thinly veiled procrastination on my part. Since most theatre programs required auditions, it made sense to visit the campuses at the same time as the auditions.

I put down my pen and looked at the *Seussical* script and Sort of Short List on my desk with a happy sigh. Mayzie was settled. I would keep working on my college applications tomorrow and finish them up by Sunday night hopefully.

But my happy sigh was followed by a confused groan. Now that my future was under control, I had to face the question that had lurked for days. What about Alex?

Had he broken up with me? I thought so but wasn't sure. Like he threatened last week, he started driving to school, leaving me alone on the bus. When I was free, he was at soccer – the boys team was having its best year ever, making it to the state final which was tomorrow. When he was free, I was in rehearsal. When we were both home, my parents watched us like nervous hawks. He wasn't texting me and I didn't have the stomach to text him and be ignored.

Sneaking into his room was a non-starter. I tried one night a while ago, but the second I raised my hand to the doorknob Mom appeared in the hallway like some kind of Harry Potter-ish wraith. I had immediately turned to the stairs, putting my raised hand on the rail, and gone down to the kitchen for a drink.

Now, I'd gone basically two days without even seeing him for a second. I had to find a way to talk to him. I dug up the courage to text.

SADIE: WHAT'S OUR STATUS?

ALEX: STATUS? WE'RE NOT A PROJECT.

At least he wasn't ignoring my texts like he'd been ignoring me face to face.

SADIE: SORRY. MY MOM SAID THE DOCTORS THINK MAYBE THEY FOUND THE CURE FOR YOUR MOM. THAT'S GREAT.

ALEX: WE'LL SEE IF IT WORKS.

SADIE: I HOPE IT DOES.
SADIE. CAN WE PLEASE TALK?
ALEX: HOW?

Good, he didn't say no. We agreed the safest meeting place and time was at Adrienne's in a few hours. Her parents were going out.

Until then, I would try to work on my future some more.

*A*drienne had to nuke our plans because her parents cancelled their plans. I couldn't stand to wait another day. Alex suggested we ask Lucey if we could go to her house, which was a short walk from Adrienne's. I'd never understand how he stayed friends with her. I didn't trust her to keep our secret so I broke down and asked Kristina for help, after telling her about me and Alex.

At four thirty, Alex bounced through the door to Kristina's kitchen, inappropriately happy for the situation, but that was better than being depressed or mad. Kristina grabbed her coconut water from the counter and left us alone. I couldn't believe she and I were enemies until last spring.

"Alex, I asked Ms. English for help with Mayzie last week and it worked. More important, I learned something." I looked at his hand hanging by his side, but didn't take it.

"You set up this meeting so we could talk about the show?" He tilted his head and gave me a green squint.

"Please, let me talk. Sorry if I don't make sense. You know I don't do well without a script." He gave a sweet smirk and nodded. "So what I learned was that asking for what I want, and what I need, isn't so bad after all. And I don't want to lie in bed every night with you across the hallway, wondering if we're broken up for real or dating but pretending to be broken up or what. So I'm asking you – what are we?"

Two second pause. "What do you want us to be?" he asked.

Moment of truth. Do it, Sadie. "I want us to be together. Of course."

"Me too. So that's solved."

I sighed relief and frustration. "But I'm so sick of our charade. Our *Midsummer Night's Dream* is more like A Mid-Autumn Nightmare. I really don't think acting like we hate each other is healthy." God, why did I sound so whiny?

"Then you'll be happy to hear my news." The smile I now realized he'd been containing since he walked in stretched across his face. "My mom is getting better. Finally! The new drugs are working. Which means–"

"–that soon she'll be home and you can get the hell out of my house. Yea!"

"And I can get the hell out of your house." We laughed as he picked me up and spun me around. In my head, the sun came out from behind a massive cloud and a choir of angels began to sing.

"God, I hate having you there. Can I just say that now? Can you, like, not come back for a really long time?" I asked between laughs.

"Please. You're a horrible sister or roommate or whatever it is your parents think you are to me now. You take more time in the bathroom than anyone I've ever known."

"That's just cause you've never had a sister. I am not that bad compared to some girls!"

Our laughs calmed down to the occasional giggle.

"And, guess what? The police have dropped all charges. They said the eyewitness proved to be unreliable." He beamed.

"Oh, Alex, I'm so happy for you! Everything is getting back to normal, finally." I hugged him ferociously.

"But we're not out of the woods yet," Alex said, pulling back. "The doctors still want to keep her in the hospital a few more weeks, maybe even a whole month they said, to make sure she's really getting better, and isn't contagious anymore. So we can't screw up our little drama now. Not when we've got this far."

"Don't you think now we could–"

"No! I've thought of that too. If we let on that this whole thing was a lie on our part, your parents will be pissed. I don't want them to hate me. Or you."

"And if we tell them we just started going out again, we'll still have the issue of them not wanting us in the same house." He nodded. I bit my lip. "Maybe I could get a chastity belt to reassure them," I joked. Alex raised an eyebrow at me. "Ugh, fine, it's on with the show. This has been my least favorite acting gig of all time. Hey, do you think I can put this on my college applications? 'Played the role of heartbroken and angry ex-girlfriend for an awe-inspiring and extended length of time'?"

"Yeah, no. Anyway, it will definitely be easier to keep the act going knowing the end is really in sight. We just have to keep thinking of each other like brother and sister, or pretend the other one is someone really annoying that you can't stand."

"Okay. And I promise not to get mad or wonder if you're serious when you're a jerk to me."

"Back at you, babe." We laughed again. "Hey, remember when you said on the bus that time that you felt like people around us could tell we're still together? Because of the electricity between us or something?" I nodded. "Why do you think your parents don't notice that?" he asked.

I looked at the ceiling and pondered. "I guess at the end of the day, we're only bit players in my household. They're too busy with their own stuff to really notice us. Or maybe they don't want to see."

"Or, maybe we're just that good at acting," Alex said. "I know I am," he said smugly, surprising me.

"Oh really, Olivier?"

"I'm that good, because I learned from the best," he said, putting his hands on my hips and pulling me close.

"And Sadie? For the record, I've never thought of you like a sister," he said, kissing me definitively.

CHAPTER 23: NEW GENRES

I psyched myself up for the final few weeks of pretending by channeling Maria in *West Side Story*. If she and Tony could hide their forbidden love from their families, so could Alex and I. Unlike Maria and Tony, we were going to survive until the day our relationship could be public.

And we really were okay, and still going out. Just in time for Saturday's state soccer championship. I pretty much hated soccer, but I loved the goalie and there was no way I was missing his big game.

A special bus was arranged to schlep students to the game at the state university forty minutes away. "Special" because it didn't usually make this trip, not because it was a cushy, modern bus or anything.

I crammed into the old school bus with Adrienne, Tom and everyone else, wondering for the hundredth time why seat belts weren't required on school buses – a question that took on urgency when we lurched from lane to lane on the highway, our near-sighted driver having way too much fun now that he was free of Smalltown's winding roads. When snowflakes started drifting down the bus windows, the ride got even more nerve-wracking. A few flurries was nothing to most New England drivers, but flurries plus old driver plus decrepit bus equalled a fingernail-biting ride.

At last, we reached the university. The frigid air cut into my lungs when I stepped off the bus onto a light crunch of snow. Soccer in the winter. Great. I secretly thanked my mother for making me wear long underwear.

After paying admission, our busload of kids launched into the bleachers after finding our section of the stands. We were playing

Taylor High from the northeast of Massachusetts, a team we never played during the regular season, so we had no idea what to expect, or at least that's what Tom explained to me as we bounced in the stands trying not to freeze while the players warmed up on the field.

Our cheerleaders, led by Lucey, jumped around on the sidelines, encouraging the crowd to get noisy.

"Give me a C," they yelled, in what must be the oldest cheer in history. I wondered if cave men and women knew that one. Give me a C-A-V-E...The Crudup fans yelled back "C", egging the cheerleaders on to the letter "R". Adrienne gave me the evil eye because I didn't join in but I just wrinkled my nose at her. So Tom screamed "U" two inches from my face, making me cover my ears. "Do it!" he said between letters, "or I'll keep screaming at you!" He smiled evilly.

I gave in at the second "U", yelling at the top of my lungs if only to get Tom out of my face. When we finished spelling and yelling "Crudup", the crowd exploded. Adrienne wrapped her arm through mine and practically pulled me off balance with her uncontrollable jumping.

And then the game started. What can I say about it? It was cold. The crowd was ear-piercing noisy. Alex looked hotter than hot in his goalie uniform. He would have looked even better without the sweat pants under his shorts, but hey, it was freezing outside. I think our team did okay in the first half, but when the halftime buzzer blared, there was no score.

To fill the fifteen-minute intermission, I debated between walking, looking for a porta-potty or sitting down, unsure which would warm me up best, when Kristina squeezed into our group, looking extremely unhappy.

"What took you guys so long?" I asked.

"We've been here for a while but couldn't get this far into the stands. But we missed the first twenty minutes because Jocelyn got stopped for speeding."

Tom, Adrienne and I immediately grinned.

"It's not funny," Kristina admonished. "She's gonna have to pay about a thousand dollars when all the fines are done, and she loses her license for three months."

157

"Guess you should have taken the bus with the rest of us," Tom said, still smiling.

Kristina shook her head. "Tell that to Jocelyn. She *had* to drive her new car. You know." She rolled her eyes, then honed in on me.

"Hey, Sadie, can I talk to you?"

"Sure," I said automatically.

Her mittened hand tugged at my coat sleeve.

"Come on, let's walk," she said, turning to thread her way through the rows of people in front of us. I shrugged at Adrienne and followed Kristina. Maybe she wanted to tell me how I was becoming a much better friend than Jocelyn was. Maybe because I didn't have a new, fast car.

We hit the track and started walking around the soccer field. The cheerleaders were finishing a pyramid in the center of the field. Kristina let her fake-fur-trimmed hood fall over her face, almost as if she didn't want to be seen. She hadn't spoken by the time we reached the first goal.

"So, what's up?" I asked, curling my fingers up inside my mittens, the warmish heels of my hands slightly thawing my frozen fingertips.

"I think I screwed up. And I'm really sorry." She smooshed her lips together, not looking at me.

I kept walking. "What are you talking about?"

"I blabbed your secret. I didn't mean to, really." She walked faster.

We were coming up behind the Crudup team, huddled on the ground in their red-and-tan uniforms. Alex was easy to pick out of the group in his black goalie shirt with the red number seven on the back. "Oh my God. Alex? My Alex secret?" The cold air stung my lungs with fresh bite. All that effort on our part to keep it quiet until the end, and Kristina messed it all up? "Who did you tell?"

She didn't answer but turned so I saw her face. Her gaze crossed the field to where the cheerleaders were jumping around on the sideline and drinking hot chocolate or coffee or something to stay warm.

"One of the cheerleaders? Oh my God. Not Lucey. Kristina, tell me you didn't tell Lucey!" Kristina's silence was my answer. "Why the hell did you do that?!" I demanded, immediately feeling guilty for jumping ugly when I saw Kristina's eyes getting wet.

She heaved a sigh, propelling a massive wave of fog into the air in front of her. "This is what happened. So we were hanging at her house last night, for the first time in a while, and she started opening up to me about, you know, the pregnancy."

"Oh, wow. Really?"

"Yep. You know she's never told anyone much about it. Not even me or Jocelyn. So she talked for a while, about being pregnant, about being ashamed, about how putting the baby up for adoption was the hardest thing she's ever done. Even harder than actually giving birth, she says." She paused to pull a stray piece of hair out of her mouth.

"Keep going," I said.

"So then we started talking about life getting back to normal for her, and how she finally felt like she was getting past the whole pregnancy thing. And then she says she wants to have a normal boyfriend relationship. And that she's really into Alex, and do I think he would go out with her."

"Oh."

"I played along for a while, Sadie, really I tried. But she'd been crying and was all sad and vulnerable, and then she finally cheered up when she talked about Alex, and I just didn't want her to get hurt or disappointed by chasing Alex when he's not available. I mean, she has been through a lot," she trailed off.

I sighed. "So you told her about me and Alex."

"Not exactly. Not at first. I tried to convince her not to go after him. But she thought it was because I liked him. Then she thought I was saying he wouldn't want to go out with her, and she started getting mad. And then she started crying again. So finally, I told her that he wouldn't be interested because he was still going out with you." She looked at me for the first time. "I'm sorry, Sadie. You probably hate me now."

My head started to throb. "I don't hate you, Kristina, but what am I going to do? You know she'll tell other people and then my father will find out when the kids at school start talking about it. I'm screwed." I rubbed my forehead with the heel of my hand.

"Maybe she won't say anything about it." Kristina winced when I cast my best skeptical look upon her. "I know. I know. Of course she'll say something."

The world's loudest horn blared and the two teams ran onto the field while the crowd erupted. Kristina and I were back at the stands. I moved my stiff legs up the bleacher steps toward Tom and Adrienne.

"I think I'll stand over there with Jocelyn," Kristina said quietly as I walked away.

*T*he second half was even more of a blur to me than the first half. My brain was as numb as my fingers and toes after Kristina's revelation. Between the stinging cold and the fear of being discovered and getting into trouble, my eyes kept tearing up. I had a hard time following the progress of the game, but counted on Tom's reactions to clue me in. When he cheered, I cheered. When he groaned, I groaned.

I did manage to watch Alex make save after save. It seemed like the other team was pummeling him this half, and I didn't know how he kept the ball out of the net. Sure enough, after two straight shots in a row, Taylor High scored. Alex leaped up to the corner of the goal but the ball went past his fingertips into the net. He fell to the ground and huddled up small, his head down.

"Somebody comfort him!" I screamed in my head. "Tell him it's okay." But Alex's teammates were running away from him.

"What are they doing? Where are they going?" I yelled at Tom.

"It's okay, Sadie, the coach called a time out." Tom yelled back patiently. "Don't worry, we'll get it back," he added, although he looked worried himself.

While the team huddled on the sideline, I thought about how Alex used the CDC as a distraction from his problems. It would be a relief to focus on something besides the Kristina-Lucey-Alex situation. I immersed myself in the game atmosphere, willing Alex's teammates to score and redeem him. I still didn't have a clue what was happening on the field, but I could feel a difference in the crowd's intensity. The tension was thicker than the cold as the clock ticked down. Fifteen minutes to go. Ten.

Suddenly, the crowd roared and the Crudup fans started yelling bloody murder. I couldn't understand a word, but their anger turned to excitement when the referee held up a yellow card.

"Yes! Yes!" Tom screamed, high-fiving Adrienne.

"What is it? What is it?" I yelled to Adrienne, barely able to hear myself.

"Penalty kick, I think." She turned to Tom and yelled into his ear. "Is it, Tom?"

"Yes! Penalty kick!" he screamed at us. "Their sweeper tripped Jake in the penalty box, so we get a penalty kick. Yes!!!!" he roared like a deranged lion.

Adrienne and I stared at him and then each other. Shrugging, we grinned and started shouting with everyone else while the players ran into a formation I'd never seen before.

An amazing quiet crept over the stands as Jake set up the ball for his penalty kick. Just him and the goalie from Taylor High. One player against another. I was so glad it wasn't the other way around, with Alex being shot upon by the other team. While we waited for Jake's kick, I noticed that every flake of snow was gone from the field, pulverized by twenty-two pairs of stampeding soccer shoes.

Jake took three steps and thwacked the ball. Like a bullet it went to the upper right corner of the goal, just like the shot that got past Alex earlier in the half.

"Hah! Take that!" I yelled, caught up in the passion of the match for real.

Alex ran up to the middle of the field to congratulate Jake but quickly sped back to his goal. Time was running out.

WIth the score tied, the two teams fought like gladiators. Or like there was no tomorrow. Or something intense and fierce – my sports references were basically non-existent. They fought like it was their final performance. Which it was.

Neither team kept the ball for long before the other team took it away. To the left of us, the Taylor fans cheered while we moaned, then they'd go quiet while we cheered. It was like the fans were having their own match on the sidelines.

Suddenly, everyone around me began jumping, making me clutch Adrienne's arm for balance.

"Lindsay's got the ball!" she shrieked.

He was the only one around – how did that happen? – except for the Taylor goalie, who crouched and shifted around trying to find the best place to wait. Three green streaks – Taylor players – bombed toward Lindsay and the goal.

"Shoot! Shoot!" yelled everyone around me. All my muscles clenched.

"One minute to go in regular time," the announcer said, barely audible over the fans.

"Shoot!" I yelled.

Lindsay took an eternity, getting as close to the goalie as possible. Finally, the goalie launched himself at Lindsay. At the same time, Lindsay tapped the ball past the goalie's left side. The ball didn't go very far and the goalie scrambled back into position but Lindsay zipped around the goalie and got the ball first. He gave it a solid kick and launched it into the middle of the goal. OH MY GOD!!!! We did it! Crudup High won the State Soccer Championship!

Fifteen. Fourteen. Thirteen. The announcer counted down the final seconds, the crowd counting with him in raspy voices.

I got caught up in a flood of people moving down the bleachers, petrified I was going to get pushed or trip.

"What are we doing?" I asked Adrienne.

"Come on!" she yelled, leaping down the final step and swarming onto the field with everyone else.

"Three. Two. One!"

As the final horn blared, the Crudup students, parents and other fans surrounded our team, each player the center in a pod of people. Tom, Adrienne and I found Lindsay and hugged him all together. I got someone's elbow in my ear but didn't care. When Lindsay was torn away from our pod by another pod, I noticed he'd left a dark sweat mark on my bright red parka.

I looked down the field for Alex, in time to see Lucey literally jump into his arms, wrapping her legs around his torso so he had no choice but to hold her, or let her fall which he'd never do. She smothered his cheeks with kisses. What the–?

Alex twisted out from under Lucey and jogged toward us, high-fiving fans along the way. When he reached our group, he hesitated for a second, plowed into us and wrapped his arms around me, Adrienne and Tom in one big group hug. In our impromptu huddle, I was free to inhale his sweaty mountain breeze smell and absorb his special-for-me smile, which was as good as any kiss.

"See you guys later!" he said, and broke away to hug the next group of friends.

After circling around in a daze for a while, we headed back to the bus. I seriously thought I had frostbite on my fingers and toes. Wasn't anyone else as cold as me? The heat on the bus washed over me and brought my digits back to throbbing, painful life.

Even though my muscles ached from the cold, I grinned as I plopped down on the seat,. Tom and Adrienne fake argued over who got the window seat in the row behind me. When they were settled, Tom leaned forward to be heard over the hubbub on the bus. "What do you think, Sadie? Soccer's not so bad after all, is it?" he said, wiping a black glove under his thawing nose.

I peeled off a mitten and exhaled on my red fingers. "Actually, Tom, you know what?" I said, cocking my head to the right. "That was a really good show."

CHAPTER 24: INTERFERENCE

*A*fter the high of the soccer game, I was shocked to experience what felt like post-event letdown the next week. I thought that only happened with theatre.

But I managed to get all my college applications in the mail, in time for the deadlines. Now, I had to wait to hear about audition dates and times.

Alex and I snuck in more smiles and quick hand-holdings when we were around Adrienne, Tom or Kristina, to hold us until the charade was officially over.

On a regular basis, I daydreamed about telling my parents the truth, but I always ended up back where Alex and I left it. It wasn't worth the risk of my parents realizing we'd been playing them all this time. Definitely better to pretend Alex and I got back together after Mrs. Holman came home. That was unless Lucey sabotaged us and starting talking. So far, for some unknown reason, she'd kept quiet about our secret.

Rehearsals entered the crisis phase. The last week before Tech Week and still so much to do. Ms. English scheduled rehearsals every day.

I tested out my new Mayzie and she worked! I'd finally found her essence, and I loved her more than ever, now that I understood her flaws. Foster gave me a big hug after "Mayzie in Palm Beach" at Wednesday's rehearsal. "Nailed it," he said, giving me a huge smile.

Once I got Mayzie down, my attention wandered to the rest of *Seussical*, wanting to help out with other parts of the show like I'd done for *Wuthering Heights* and *Twilight* junior year. But everywhere I turned, looking to have input, there was a parent. Mrs. Madison and Mrs. Freedman on costumes. Mrs. Carter, Mr.

Fishbein and Mr. Kent on set design and props. A bunch of other mothers floating around constantly, helping I guess with ticket sales, program design, and all the other stuff we used to do ourselves or not do at all.

I guess with all that help, we should have been in good shape acting-wise, only having ourselves to worry about. But Lindsay still didn't know all his lines. Everyone in the cast was getting annoyed with him. He got defensive instead of getting serious about reading his script.

The rest of us were okay, except for a few middle schoolers who kept goofing off until Foster threatened to hang them out the second floor window by their feet if they didn't get their shit together. Ms. English said she was pleased with their improved attitude, not having a clue how it happened

Then there was the pit band nightmare. We only had a few days before we should be rehearsing with real musicians, since Ms. English insisted we'd have a live band this year instead of recorded music. But still, no band. Ms. English tried to sweet-talk the band director into helping out but he didn't have a lot of good student musicians to draw from in our small school, and she didn't want to pay professional musicians.

Meanwhile, the parents kept having inane arguments over where to put the band since we didn't have a true pit. House right, house left. How about on the stage itself, upstage behind a sheer curtain like in a production of *Chicago* Mrs. Carter raved about? Should they have microphones or would that be too loud? Should they be screened in, to dampen the sound? How many musicians should we even have?

Worst of all, the parents had officially hijacked stage crew from Adrienne, even though she had Tom and a few other kids lined up to help. In the end, she told them all except Tom not to bother, because Mrs. Carter announced she had plenty of parents to work backstage, not to mention snazzy little lanyards for the stage crew to wear so they would be allowed backstage by whatever security she thought we had. If the parents weren't so annoying, they'd be funny.

At Thursday's rehearsal, we reached our breaking point. Mrs. Madison kept interrupting us backstage to double-check our waist or girth or whatever with her measuring tape. A gaggle of parents making fish cut-outs at the side of the stage kept chattering, making it hard to hear. And in the wings, the parent "helpers" kept getting in the way, making Adrienne and Tom miss a bunch of cues and dragging out the set changes so long that Ms. English complained a few times.

Something had to change.

"*H*ey, Ms. English, how do you think the show's looking?" Tom asked innocently after everyone else left the auditorium.

She stopped jamming her libretto and score into her bag and looked at us as if we'd asked how many miles it was to the moon.

"Well," she said, standing up straight, "I guess it's okay, but we've got a lot of bugs to work out still." She looked from Tom to Adrienne to me. "Why? How do *you* think it's going?"

"We're a little worried about the music," Tom said. "We know you really want a full band, and that would be cool, but we're running out of time to find people and have them learn the songs."

"Yes, but you know how I feel about using a boom box. Very unprofessional." She turned back to her bag, struggling to get the wayward documents into a bulging compartment.

"Tom has another idea," Adrienne said.

Ms. English kept her attention on her bag. "Okay, Tom, let's hear it."

"There's this kid in eighth grade, Patrick, who's a piano whiz."

"He's a prodigy, not just a whiz," Adrienne interjected.

"Yeah, he could learn the entire show in one day, I bet," Tom said. "And he'd be able to follow along with the cast like you wanted the band to, slowing down or speeding up to stay with them and keep them on tempo." He looked at Adrienne, giving her the floor.

"Best of all, he already knows some of the *Seussical* songs."

"Really?" Ms. English asked. "Has he worked on the show before?"

"He was our accompanist for *Whossical*," I said, unable to stay quiet.

166

"Oh, that boy. He was really good. Okay, I'm game. Ask him to come see me tomorrow in my room." She picked up her bag to leave but saw us rooted to the floor. "Was there something else?"

"It's just that, well, it's a little crowded backstage, to be honest. Lots of helpers running around, if you know what I mean," Adrienne said.

"You mean you have *too* many stage crew? That's a first," Ms. English said, eyes wide.

"Mm, maybe just not the right ones," Tom said, taking a deep breath. "They've never done this, after all, and everyone's a little confused, and no one's really in charge."

"Mrs. Carter is supposed to be in charge. Isn't she?"

"I guess," Adrienne said.

Long, awkward pause. Maybe I could help.

"Adrienne could run stage crew, you know. I mean, she's done it for all our other shows, and she's the best at it."

Ms. English grimaced in sympathy. "Adrienne, having watched you all fall I'm sure you do a bang-up job with stage crew. But I have to play politics here. I've got all these parent volunteers wanting to help out, and we wouldn't have the show we're going to have without them. I have to let them do the jobs they want to do." She frowned at our fallen faces.

"Can't you just work with them, and make sure everything goes smoothly? You know, sort of work around them?"

"You wouldn't mind? If we just do our thing?" Adrienne asked, a glimmer of hope in her voice.

"I don't mind. Obviously you can't be rude or anything. Listen to what Mrs. Carter says, and do what she asks, but also go ahead and fix things or do it your way if you know that's better. Without being rude." She nodded as if that made perfect sense, before walking away.

Tom and Adrienne looked like I felt. "I guess that's a victory. Sort of," I muttered.

Exit all.

I'd never realized how much pageantry, ceremony and, well, showmanship sports had. At the championship game, I'd noticed the team huddling and yelling something before they ran onto the field. The formal announcer, the competing cheerleaders doing halftime routines, and the player formations that broke apart at the referee's whistle – they were all rituals that added – there was no other word for it – drama, to the game.

I had a similar feeling walking into the Crudup gym the Saturday night after the soccer team won states. This was the first sports banquet I'd ever been to. It was the first school sports event of any kind I'd ever been to, unless you counted watching the soccer games I didn't understand and attending a bunch of in-school pep rallies, not by choice.

But I liked the aura in the gym as I walked in with my parents, of course not with Alex who had driven alone. Our gymnasium had been transformed into a restaurant for the celebration dinner. White tablecloths glowed and forks and knives gleamed under the fluorescent lights. A long row of shiny trophies lit up the center table. Red and tan streamers floated from the rafters and every inch of wall was covered with posters saying "We're #1" and "Bravest of the Braves".

"There's Alex," Mom said, pointing across the gym as we worked our way to an empty table. "Alex!" she yelled, to my horror. He looked over, grimacing what he probably meant as a smile, and moved toward us. I stole a look, figuring I was entitled since my mother just announced her interest in him to the entire Crudup community. He was in a pale yellow dress shirt and dark blue tie. Green would have highlighted his eyes better, but still he was gorgeous. I liked casual Alex better than buttoned-up Alex, but he did clean up good, his blonde hair combed to the side and his face obviously just shaved.

While I soaked him in, he focused on my mother as he walked up.

"Hi Mrs. Perkins. Mr. Perkins," he said, nodding at my dad who reached out a hand.

"Congratulations, Alex. I know I see you every day at home, but I officially want to say great job. You've gone from barely making the team to star goalie. You must feel pretty good about that," he said, pumping Alex's hand. Their hands were the same size, I noticed.

"John," Mom said on cue. Honestly, I could script their conversations sometimes. "Must you ruin the moment by mentioning the less than stellar early athletic years?" she said, not making it better.

Alex smiled at her reassuringly. "It's okay, he's right. I guess it does make tonight even better, coming so far in two years." He didn't even look at me. "Well, I've gotta go."

"But why don't you sit with us since your mother couldn't come?" Mom asked.

"I, um–"

"Wendy, let the boy sit with the team. He doesn't want to sit with us," Dad said, glancing quickly at me.

"It's not that," Alex said, straightening his tie unnecessarily. "But we're supposed to sit together. See? That long table is for all the players. So, okay. See you later." And he left us.

Adrienne, my savior as usual, popped up behind me. "Hey, Sadie, want to sit together? Come on, Tom and I are over there." I looked at my mother who nodded, not that I was asking permission.

"We'll see you after the banquet," she said, pushing a lock of auburn hair behind her ear. "Oh look, John, the Houstons are here. Let's go say hi."

After Adrienne and I escaped to a table near the locker room door, I saw the cheerleaders hovering in the hallway, their high-pitched chatter ping-ponging into the gym. I swear, to be a cheerleader, your voice had to have a higher than normal pitch. Or maybe the role came first, and afterward your voice underwent this non-surgical change.

Why was my father walking into the middle of the cheerleaders? Must be going to the bathroom in that hallway. Oh God, he was walking right by Lucey. And she was talking to him! I froze, willing myself to suddenly have super-human hearing or the ability to read lips. No secret powers came to my rescue. All I could do was watch their pantomime against the columns of dirty, beige lockers.

"Sadie, are you listening?" Adrienne asked, following my glance. "Oh. Not good."

I'd told Adrienne, Tom and Alex about Kristina's screw-up, but no one had any great ideas for how to keep Lucey quiet. Alex tried talking to her but she'd made it clear she had no interest in talking about me. I think that finally made him start to change his opinion of Lucey.

"You know," Adrienne said soothingly. "Maybe it's not a big deal if your parents find out. You can't help it if you like each other. And they like Alex."

Since Dad had moved out of view, I slowly shifted my gaze to Adrienne. "I've been lying to them all fall. I've been lying to them for three entire months. Living a lie. Under their roof. All they've ever asked of me is to not–"

"Okay, okay, I get it. Jeesh. I was just trying to make you feel better. Let's talk about something else."

We ate, and listened to speeches, and applauded mechanically, and watched the cheerleaders do a special routine, and the players accept their trophies. The whole time, I wondered what Lucey had said to my Dad. She'd love to get me in trouble. Maybe she thought if my parents knew I'd been lying, they would pull me from the show, opening up the part of Mayzie for, I don't know, Lucey? But my parents would never do that. I'd have to do something a lot worse for them to pull the plug on my oxygen supply.

CHAPTER 25: HERPES SIMPLEX

𝓛ucey was like a cold sore that kept coming back at the worst time, threatening to ruin my last year of high school. Just when things were going smoothly, there she was again, finding some way to make me miserable.

As the banquet clatter and chatter faded into the background, my brain shifted into overdrive, thinking up different ways Lucey might have told my dad about me and Alex.

"You must be so proud of your daughter's boyfriend, Mr. Perkins."

"That Alex is so great. And Alex and Sadie. What a cuuute couple!"

"Must be tough keeping Alex out of Sadie's bedroom since they're so serious about each other."

"You are so progressive to let your daughter's boyfriend live in your house, on the same floor, across the hall, steps away--"

The pumpkin pie I'd eaten for dessert flip-flopped in my stomach in a threatening way. I leaped up, my napkin falling to the floor. Tom and Adrienne raised their eyebrows at me while the soccer coach droned on at the microphone.

"Bathroom," I mouthed. "Be right back." Tom nodded. Adrienne smiled.

I heaved open the swinging bathroom door and almost ran into the obnoxious cold sore.

```
                  SADIE

        'Scuse me.

        (Rolls her eyes at her inability to come
        up with a scathing comment.)
```

LUCEY

It's Sadie! The Crudup slut.

SADIE

(Winces.)

What-- What are you talking about?

LUCEY

You know. Living with your boyfriend and all. On top of last summer, when you attacked Luke at theatre camp. Never thought you had it in you.

(Tugs at her cheerleader sweater and primps as if someone who cares is watching.)

SADIE

What-- How-- You know I didn't attack Luke. And you even said I <u>should</u> date him, because he was so rich and handsome and all. 'Have a fling' you said, remember? When you were pretending to be my friend.

(Touch of relief crosses her face at having found her voice.)

LUCEY

Yeah but I didn't realize how serious Alex was about you then. How could you do that to him? Oh well, I guess you're making it up to him now. What do you guys do, wait until your parents are asleep and then you crawl through his window or something?

(Like she's musing.)

Very Twilight-ish.

(SADIE winces again.)

That's right. I know your little secret. That you and Alex are fooling your parents into thinking you're broken up so you can live together. Very risqué. I'm actually a little impressed.

                    SADIE

You are? Wait-- you're wrong. Alex and I are <u>not</u> going out. I don't know what you heard but it's not true. We broke up ages ago.

                    LUCEY

Really? Oh good. So you'll have no problem if I date him. 'Cause he is <u>really</u> hot, and I think we'd make the perfect couple. I don't know which is hotter, his face or his bod. Personality's not bad either, if you're into the nice guy sort of thing. I bet he's an amazing kisser. Can't wait to find out.

(Exit LUCEY.)

What just happened? I didn't even find out if she'd said anything to my father. It seemed like she was more interested in getting Alex to ask her out than in getting me in trouble. I should have figured that out. I didn't enter into Lucey's thoughts unless I could get her something she wanted. In this case, by refusing to admit Alex and I were still a couple, I gave her the opening to go after Alex.

Which she continued doing. Relentlessly. Starting right after the banquet.

"Alex, you have to come to the party at my house!" she begged him as the dinner broke up, parents and teachers making for the door and students hanging back trying to figure out how to keep the celebration going. "Everyone's coming and you're the star of the game! You have to be there. What else are you going to do?" she said, staring right at me and rubbing against him like some red and tan cat.

"Come on, Holman, we'll never win states again," Lindsay pointed out.

"Yeah, you gotta come, dude," said Jake.

Alex looked at me and I nodded ever so slightly. He had to go. He'd only win states once. I turned away quickly so he wouldn't see my eyes welling up.

Could these last few weeks of pretending to be broken up suck any more? Was it really worth it? I moved toward the door.

"Sade, do you want to go to the party?" Adrienne asked, catching up with me.

"No, I don't think so. It's too awkward. I'm gonna find my parents and get a ride home with them." I started to trudge off.

"Okay. Sorry you can't come. Talk to you later."

I turned back. "Wait, you guys are going?" She nodded. "Keep an eye on him for me, okay? Make sure he doesn't have a beer. He can't drink with the medicine he's on." Adrienne nodded. "And her. Keep an eye on you know who." My voice hitched.

"I will. I'll tell you everything. And don't worry."

As I walked out of the school, a crowd of jostling, shouting kids caught my eye. Lucey was attached to Alex like a barnacle. My heart stung like it had frostbite.

Somehow I slept, like a teenager with no life. I didn't even hear Alex come home.

Surprisingly early the next morning, my phone chirped with a text. It was him.

ALEX: HEY.
SADIE: HEY. HAVE FUN LAST NIGHT?
ALEX: SORT OF. MISSED YOU.
SADIE: YOU DID?
ALEX: LOTS. SADIE?

SADIE: WHAT
ALEX: I REALLY LOVE YOU.
I kissed my phone.
SADIE: I LOVE YOU TOO.

CHAPTER 26: SLEEPING BUTT

With soccer season officially over and Mrs. Holman cleared to come home the week of the show, *Seussical* became the main topic of conversation in my house, and not a minute too soon as Tech Week was here. At dinner, my parents asked lots of silly questions I didn't mind answering since it let me talk about the show, while Alex acted disinterested in all things Sadie even though I knew he was really hanging on every word.

Tuesday night, when everyone was in bed, I heard a small hiss in the hall. Four twelve, the clock said. I crept to my door, turned the handle in tiny increments to prevent that clicking noise, and eased my door open. Alex was framed in Jesse's doorway, wearing his favorite green T-shirt with the little frog over the pocket and blue plaid pajama bottoms, his blonde hair going in all directions. For the millionth time, I wondered how I got such a hot boyfriend.

He waved a blue can of WD-40, grinned, and walked into his room, motioning for me to follow. As soon as I crossed the threshold, he eased his squeak-less door shut as gently as I'd opened mine. Tip-toeing the three steps to the foot of the bed, cartoon-style, he put the WD-40 into his backpack there, and tip-toed back. Wrapping his arms around me, he pulled me into the warmest, coziest hug I'd ever known. He pulled back a few inches, and we kissed our first real kiss in ages.

"I don't want to push it," he breathed into my ear. "Go back to bed. But I'll meet you in your room tomorrow night, when we have more time."

"Okay. What time?" I breathed back, feeling tingly all over from his touch and the danger of being together, alone in his room, with my parents in the very next room.

He squinted as if making a huge decision. "One seventeen. Exactly." He smiled at me and I nodded.

"Okay. Bye." We snuck one more kiss and I left.

Wednesday night, I tossed and turned, trying not to look at the clock. Kato seemed to know something was up. He'd left his bed near the foot of the stairs to come into my room around midnight. At one, I stopped avoiding the clock and watched the minutes change over until one fifteen. I sensed more than heard my doorknob move in the dark. Alex's blurry shape loomed over me.

"You're two minutes early," I whispered, while Kato's tail thumped against the floor.

"Do you want me to leave and come back?" He turned to go. I reached for his retreating shape and clutched his shirt.

"No!" I stifled a giggle.

"Oh, good. I couldn't wait." He leaned over and kissed me quickly. "This is too close to the door. Let's sit over there." He grabbed my hand and towed me to the far side of the room, where we sat against the wall, immediately making out like it was our last day on Earth.

Ten minutes later, we pulled back at the same time. Definitely time to stop. He sighed and ran his hand through his hair. I straightened my T-shirt and resisted the urge to clear my throat, which I thought might be too loud. I shivered and wrapped my arms around myself.

"Wait–" Alex said, jumping to his feet and returning quickly with the orange comforter from my bed. He sat back down and tucked the comforter around us. Kato immediately padded over and lay practically on top of us, threatening to steal the entire blanket.

"Okay," Alex said, taking my hand, "tell me everything about the show. Are you guys ready? Is it going to be good? How was rehearsal today, and has Lindsay learned his lines yet?"

"You're having CDC withdrawal, aren't you?" I accused, my eyes squinting, the closest I dared get to a laugh.

"Maybe a little." He shifted closer to me. "Okay, a lot. But I'm having Sadie withdrawal more. I just want to hear your voice talking to me. So go on."

He leaned his head back against the wall and closed his eyes while I whisper rambled on about every aspect of the show. Sitting here in the dark in a position I'd never been in before, whispering so my parents wouldn't hear, my comforter trapping the warmth of our bodies, I felt weirdly at home and secure. My hushed stories lulled even me. I stopped talking a few times to see if Alex was asleep, but every time he'd open his eyes and tell me to keep going.

When I couldn't think of anything else to say, I closed my eyes.

"Shit!" Alex whispered loudly, scrambling up, my waking head falling violently off his shoulder. "Gotta go." He dropped the comforter, scurried to my door, opened it a sliver, peeked out, and slipped into Jesse's room. Kato slurped me good morning and left more leisurely. Two minutes later, my parents' door opened and my mother scuffed down the stairs to make coffee.

My butt was asleep and my neck was sore, but that was my best night sleep in months.

When you're in a show, all through the rehearsal phase, Tech Week hovers out there like a magical holy grail. You tell yourself that by the time Tech Week comes, the show will be in awesome shape, you'll be having a super fun time, and all you'll have left to do is enjoy the performances. I don't know why actors think that, because in my experience this has never happened in the history of the free world. Tech Week is always a train wreck of missed cues, forgotten lines, malfunctioning set pieces and short tempers.

The actual best thing about Tech Week was that you got to bond with your cast mates. Even though you'd spent weeks in rehearsals, theoretically together, you really didn't spend that much time hanging with your best friends. But during tech rehearsals, you got to fill in all the waiting time while the stage crew, lights and sound worked out their cues, by goofing around and acting silly. It was actually a good way to relieve the pressure of wondering if the show would suck or succeed.

Seussical Tech Week came and went like every other Tech Week before it. Things broke. Things got fixed. Technical cues were learned. Staging cues were perfected. We survived. Then it was show time. Do or die time.

CHAPTER 27: PRE-SHOW JITTERS

I was so excited at school Friday I couldn't concentrate on any of my classes. The *who, who wah dah* beginning of "Horton Hears A Who" ran through my head non-stop. Every time I saw Foster, he'd toss out a great *Seussical* line, about a person being a person, or biggest blame fool, or thinking thinks.

Ms. English was right, in the end. *Seussical* was an awesome show. I loved the message, the characters, the dialogue, and the songs. And we were just about ready. Lindsay was finally on top of his game, and his Cat in the Hat was hilarious. We would kick butt in our "Mayzie in Palm Beach" scene.

Actually, all the leads were going to rock. Ben as Horton, Emily as Gertrude, Kelly White as the Sour Kangaroo, Foster and Kristina and Mr. and Mrs. Mayor, and the eighth grader Max doing JoJo was doing great. When Lucey, Jocelyn and Aimee practiced their Bird Girl harmonies, I got chills a few times.

The set ended up cartoony enough, I guess, although you can never be too cartoony with Seuss. Our clover was appropriately sized, and the kettle with "fire" made of that clear plastic material for the "boil it" scene was pretty cool.

We'd tried a few different make-up approaches for the Nool creatures during Tech Week – the students and parents even working together, amazingly, until we found the best ones.

The costumes were the most elaborate we'd ever had. A zebra, lion, tiger, leopard and other assorted jungle creatures looked fantastic in plush, head-to-toe costumes that would have been laughable like kiddie pajamas if they weren't so well made. The only problem was, they were so heavy, everyone sweated to death onstage, and we didn't have time to dry clean the body odor out of them before show time. Mrs. Madison had handed out travel sized deodorants to all the jungle animals at Thursday's dress rehearsal, making a lame threat to not help with next year's show if people didn't use them.

My costume was fabulous. Hot pink and red sequins, satin and feathers. My long hair was curled tightly with the front pieces pulled back into a feathery headdress. Red fishnet stockings ended where my beige jazz shoes began. Ms. English had paid special attention to my make-up, and the result was awesome – pink and red accented with orange, purple and black, a sea of swirls, curlicues and swishes, which neatly camouflaged the huge zit on my chin. I had been expecting feathery make-up, but I loved the almost paisley effect she created. The colors somehow even made my boring brown eyes look pretty. I never thought I'd feel so gorgeous as an animal.

The Bird Girls complemented me in their blue, purple and green outfits and matching make-up, similar to mine but not quite as amayzing.

Like he did every year, Foster complained about having stage make-up on his skin, swearing it made him break out like nobody's business. Sam and I linked arms with Foster, dragged him into the handicapped unisex bathroom, and stood him between us as we looked in the mirror. Sam pointed to his black, brown and white feathered Vlad Vladikoff face, then to my pink, purple and black swirly face, and finally to Foster's lightly made up face. All his Mr. Mayor role required was some natural colored foundation, eyeliner, and red circles on his cheeks.

"Dude, are you done complaining?" Sam asked. "If anyone's going to break out here, it's us raptors."

"Hey, who are you calling a raptor? Mayzie's not a bird of prey," I objected.

"She's not? Are you sure about that?" Foster said, laughing and high-fiving Sam. They detached themselves from me and walked off together. I wasn't sure if their developing relationship was friends or more, but either way it was adorable.

Ben's costume was hysterical, all gray and soft and cuddly, like Horton should be. His ears were so ginormous it cracked us up for days. That was another best thing about Tech Week – getting your laughs out before the real show.

And the Who hair - awesome. We even gave generous props to Mrs. Freedman for coming up with the idea of sticking a small plastic soda bottle on top of the girl Who heads, covering it with hair pulled up straight and tying it at the top. Other Whos had a million braids or ponytails sticking out, and all the Whos had rosy doll-like circles on their cheeks.

I was bummed that Professor Snyder from Yale School of Drama wasn't coming to the show. I had collected all the bits of courage floating around inside of me, mushed them into one big ball and forced myself to email and invite her to the show. After all, when I'd met her at last spring's production of *Wuthering Heights: A Modern Tragedy*, she said to keep her posted on any shows I was in. She replied to my email that she'd seen *Seussical* a thousand times but thanks for the invitation.

Sometimes these days I didn't even recognize my own reactions to things, like when her rejection didn't send me into a tailspin of despair. Maybe because someone more important was coming. Mrs. Holman was getting out of the hospital Sunday, and she'd insisted on coming to *Seussical*. Alex stopped protesting when she promised she would go home and rest right after.

My near-perfect level of pre-show contentment was shattered by, of course, Lucey. I had just finished dressing at one hour until curtain when she pranced up, looking way too pleased with herself.

"Sadie, your Dad's out front. Funny, he seemed surprised when I said it was too bad Alex wasn't in the show since you two are such a cute couple together. Haven't you told him yet?" She opened her eyes as wide as possible in fake shock, then squinted them and fake laughed for good measure. "Oh well, hope I didn't spill the beans! Good luck in the show!" And she pranced off like a deer on caffeine, her rear end wiggling with satisfaction.

I turned slowly and found Adrienne standing next to me. At least it was Adrienne and not someone who didn't know The Secret. We stared at each other for a minute, eyes round.

"Man," Adrienne finally said, "can't she go get pregnant again or something and leave the rest of us alone?" She linked her arm through mine and turned toward the Home Ec/make-up room. "Come on, you need to get feathered up."

I didn't budge. "Adrienne, I feel nauseous. This is going to bug me now, just like she wanted. But I can't concentrate on the show wondering if I'm going to get in big trouble when I get home. Do you think she finally told him?" I looked down, biting my lip.

"Who knows, but–" Adrienne stopped when Ms. English strode up.

"Sadie," she said in a concerned voice. "Lucey said you're violently ill. What's wrong? You do look a bit green."

I straightened up to my full five feet five inches. "I'm fine. I don't know what she's talking about."

She analyzed me from several feet away.

"Well, okay, if you're sure."

"She's sure. She's fine. We were just heading in for make-up," Adrienne said, linking her arm more firmly through mine.

"All right. Give me fifteen minutes for make-up though. I have to finish the Bird Girls first." She turned on her designer boots and left.

The churning in my stomach built into a tsunami. Weird. This wasn't my usual post-Lucey encounter upset stomach feeling. I knew that one well after three and a half years of high school. Slowly, I realized I wasn't scared or embarrassed or frustrated about Lucey's interference like usual. I was mad.

"Can you believe her? She's trying to throw me off and ruin my performance. Or maybe she's actually trying to get me out of the show so she can be Mayzie!" My blood started to churn in time with my stomach.

"Yeah, like that's gonna work," Adrienne said. "So we won't worry about her. What about your father? Do you want me to go find him and see if he's in a good mood or a bad one? Then we'll have some kind of idea if she really said something to him?"

I shook my head slowly. "No, whatever he's feeling toward me, he won't show it to you. He's a pretty good actor. I'm going to have to do it." Adrienne raised her eyebrows at me. "Yup. So here I go." I stood there. My feet were stuck. Adrienne shrugged as if she had no choice and gave me a tiny push. "Thanks," I said, sarcastically.

"Sorry, but what are friends for?" she said. "You're right. You might as well find out if there's a sword hanging over your head." I exhaled and headed for the lobby.

(SADIE spots DAD by a side door of the school, talking to one of the math teachers. DAD sees SADIE, breaks away from his fellow teacher and approaches his daughter.)

DAD

(Frowning.)

Hey, sweetheart, aren't you afraid someone's going to see your costume? Your skimpy little costume, I might add.

And shouldn't you be getting your make-up on?

SADIE

It's okay, I've got some time. After all, I'm one of the stars, and stars get special treatment.

(Pretends to primp a little and forces a smile.)

DAD

Okay. Well, it's going to be a great show, I'm sure. Are you excited?

(SADIE searches his hazel eyes for any sign of anger or disappointment. Nothing there but good old Dad.)

SADIE

Yeah, of course. This is my best role ever.

(Squints, clearly wondering how to find out for sure if Lucey really said something or was just fooling her.)

DAD

Well, okay, break a leg, honey.

(Stoops to wrap his arms around Sadie.)

I'm going to go find your mother.

(Stands back and watches SADIE stand there.)

Unless there's something else?

SADIE

(Realizing he's not going to give anything away, she decides to be direct.)

Dad, I have to ask you something.

(Looks in her father's eyes, then to the side.)

Did Lucey say something to you tonight about me? About me and Alex?

(Forces herself to look back at him.)

(DAD stifles a smile, then scrunches up his mouth and frowns, and finally lifts and widens his eyes, making rows of wrinkles on his brow. When Sadie was young, he would do that on purpose so she could run her fingers over the ridges on his forehead, laughing at how the bumps felt.)

                    DAD

(In a fake acting voice.)

Why, I don't know what you mean. Is
there something you want to tell me,
pumpkin?

                  SADIE

(Desperation in her voice.)

Dad, stop it! Just tell me. Did she say
something?

(DAD sighs and gets serious.)

                    DAD

Yes, Miss Landau proudly informed me
that you and Alex have been dating all
fall, and that you've been pulling the
wool over my eyes, and that she hated to
rat but thought I should know.

(His voice softens.)

Is that what you mean?

                  SADIE

(Swallows painfully and nods. Tries to
mask the tears in her voice with
sincerity.)

Are you mad?

                    DAD

Come sit down.

(DAD Walks over to an old park-type bench in the hallway, sits and waits while SADIE joins him. She shifts on the bench to face him. He takes her hands in his big, warm ones.)

Sadie. Your mother and I have known for a while that you and Alex never broke up. Or at least that if you did, you started 'going out' again.

(SADIE's brain cells shriek to a stop, stall and try to re-ignite.)

                    SADIE

You have? You did? How did you know?

                    DAD

Call it parental intuition. Mothers get all the credit for that, but fathers have it too, you know. After we drove you two home from the Senior Class Play, I told Wendy I thought something was up. I just sensed it. She started paying more attention, and we decided we were right after I heard you two whispering together upstairs one afternoon.

(SADIE sputters but nothing coherent comes out.)

Mind you, I wasn't too happy when I smelled WD-40 the other morning. We almost sent Alex down to sleep on the couch that night. I didn't get a lot of sleep knowing Jesse's creaky door wouldn't wake me up if you guys tried anything foolish. On the other hand, that door has really needed to be oiled for years. I decided to follow Alex's lead and put some on my door too. That way, I could slip out and check on you guys if I had--

SADIE

Dad! All that acting we did. All that energy we put into not showing that we liked each other. All that-- all that..."

(She finishes weakly.)

DAD

(Grinning.)

I know. And your acting skills are developing very nicely, I might add. And what about us? Don't we deserve a little credit for our acting skills, not letting on that we knew?

(He smirks and cocks his head, making Sadie love him and hate him at the same time.)

SADIE

I can't believe you knew!

(Bangs her knees together a few times.)

Why didn't you say something? You let us suffer all that time!

DAD

Think about it, just for once, from our perspective. If we'd told you that we knew, we'd have had to change the situation, and Alex would have had to go to California or some foster home. We couldn't do that to him. We knew how important it was -- it is -- for him to

be near his mother while she's in the
hospital.

SADIE

Hmm. So you didn't want to admit the
truth either

(Cautiously.)

You were lying too, in a way.

DAD

Let's just say we were willing to
<u>pretend</u> we didn't know the truth. We
were perfectly willing to admit the
truth to ourselves, just not to you and
Alex. It seemed safer that way.

SADIE

(Nervously twirling a long curl around
her finger.)

What do you mean?

DAD

(Sighs.)

Someday, you'll be a parent and you'll
understand. It's like this. If you
thought we didn't know, you'd keep the
charade going and be on your best
behavior. No kissing, so sneaking around
to see each other, not even any hand
holding. Just the way I like it.

(He grins again, but drops the grin
quickly.)

If you two were willing to go to all
that effort to keep Alex in our house,

then we didn't want to interfere in your little play. After all, it was for a noble reason, right?

SADIE

(Uncertainly.)

Of course.

DAD

(Circles his hand in the air, encouraging Sadie along.)

You did it because...you were concerned for Mrs. Holman. Not, I'm sure, because you wanted to be close to your boyfriend. You would never lie to us just to do that, would you.

SADIE

Oh, no, Dad, no, that's wasn't it. I <u>hated</u> having Alex in Jesse's room. I still do! I may love him but I'm not ready to live with him.

(SADIE's mouth goes dry and her cheeks flame as she realizes she just told her father she is in love.)

(A flurry of emotions cross DAD's face.)

DAD

Hm. Well. (Buying time.)

I will say this for you and Alex. If you could put that much effort into playing a role to keep him near his mother, then you have a very strong, cooperative relationship. And I'm proud of you for supporting him like that.

(Stands up.)

Now come on, you have a show to do.

(SADIE stands up and gives him a careful hug so her costume isn't crushed, the frenzy in her mind finally slowing.)

SADIE

Dad? Thanks.

DAD

(Speaking into her hair.)

You're welcome.

(SADIE pulls back and starts to walk away.)

(DAD calls after her in his trying-to-be-funny-when-the-situation-doesn't-call-for-it-voice.)

And I like Alex a lot, too, by the way.

CHAPTER 28: IT'S SHOWTIME (SEUSSICAL)

"*G*o, bananas, go go bananas," we whispered, crouching down on the band room floor, gathered in a circle, five minutes before curtain. "Go, bananas, go go bananas," we repeated in our speaking voice, standing taller but still with bent knees. "Go, bananas, go go bananas," we yelled, jumping straight up and throwing our fists in the air.

A few months ago, I would have thought Ms. English's idea of a pre-show cheer was stupid, but I'd changed my mind about her and her methods in the past few weeks. And the camaraderie of going bananas was actually kind of fun.

Ms. English told us how proud she was and what a great job we were going to do, reminded us to enunciate and project, and left for the stage to welcome the crowd.

This was it. Time to be amayzing.

*T*he spotlight comes up on Max Bernstein, our JoJo, in a bright green T-shirt, blue jeans and yellow Converse sneakers. As he starts his lines, I try telepathically willing him to be louder. The parent running sounds notices too, and soon Max's microphone is up a bit. I give silent thanks to Ms. English for renting us real sound equipment including good wireless mikes.

As JoJo talks about the red-and-white-striped hat that looks like it's perched on a bush, Lindsay – who is crouching behind the bush facing stage left – makes faces at the cast members waiting in the wings. Afraid he's going to miss his cue, I put my hands on my hips and my maddest look on my face, but he doesn't stop. I swear, if he misses his first cue–

But Lindsay suddenly looks down for two seconds and then springs up from behind the bush, white-gloved hands thrown triumphantly in the air, exactly as JoJo says "cat". Right on time.

"Look, Mommy, it's the Cat in the Hat!" a child in the audience yells, making a giggle ripple through the nearly full house.

While Lindsay and Max banter and "Oh, The Thinks You Can Think" starts, I swing my hips in time to the piano music, biding my time. At last, it's our turn. "Seuss!" we yell in unison and saunter onstage from both sides, a blast of red, blue, green, orange, yellow, pink and purple mixed with animal stripes and spots.

I move into position for my introduction, step forward and encourage the audience to think of a bird flying off on a spree, meaning me, Mayzie. I step back after my line, wondering if something was wrong with my mike because I thought I heard a slight echo when I sang my line.

After the main characters – Horton, Mr. and Mrs. Mayor, Gertrude, the Sour Kangaroo and General Schmitz, plus me – have introduced ourselves, the cast crouches as one for the scary part of the song. The stage lights dim and in a corner of my mind, I hope the little girl or boy who cheered for the Cat in the Hat isn't scared.

We sing, we swirl, we kick, we celebrate Seuss, the stage lights get colorful again, and I am loving this number. The opening all-cast song in *Seussical* is strong enough to be a finale. We are having fun and the audience feels it, reflecting our optimism and energy back at us. I'm so glad Ms. English decided to keep all of us onstage until the end of the song instead of just JoJo and the Cat, which she also tried. I want to be involved in every second of this song.

We near the end and don't even have to concentrate on the important timing of the last few bars because they feel so natural. We stop singing as the piano goes boom. "Seuss!" we yell. Boom again and heads down. Perfect.

I love Mayzie and I love this show. Words cannot explain.

*T*he awesome opening number complete, we move into "Horton Hears A Who". The Who characters exit but us Jungle of Nool citizens move upstage where we strut, lumber, preen, and stretch in the background. Horton and the Bird Girls set up the rest of the play, alternating song with Seuss-speak, as Horton spies and rescues the speck also known as the tiny world of Whoville. The Bird Girl harmonies send a chill through me, again. Damn, I hate letting Lucey and Jocelyn have any kind of positive effect on me.

The speck deposited on a clover for safekeeping, the actors break into "Biggest Blame Fool". I'm feeling the bluesy music when the Wickersham Brothers interlude comes. Oh no, why are there only two middle school boys in monkey costumes running to the middle of the stage? Where's the third one – Jimmy? Should I yell out Jimmy's line? The song will sound stupid if no one says anything there. Wickersham One does his line. Wickersham Two shouts his line. I open my mouth to say "ha ha ha" when Jimmy bounds onstage, out of breath and gasping his lines. The audience cracks up, not for the right reason. Jimmy grins like an idiot. You've got to be kidding me. I hope Ms. English gives him hell later.

The monkeys' part is over quickly, and we rock some more until the Sour Kangaroo has her Aretha moment, mis-spelling "respect" and making the audience whoop with admiration. We launch into another beat and tempo. Kristina was right when she said this is a tricky song. But like all the *Seussical* songs, the multiple tempo and key changes just feel right, so most of the cast have no problem switching to each new section. The few who can't cut it are drowned out by those of us doing it right.

Thing 1 hands Lindsay a plastic toy microphone and the Cat starts a TV reporter shtick. My next line is coming. It's coming. Here it comes.

I hog the mike and suggest everyone focus on darling me. I ace my first real singing line, feeling strong and sure, only a little distracted by Lucey entering my field of vision to my left. That's weird. The Bird Girls are supposed to stay behind me, like back-up singers.

Too soon, the number is over. Up next is my least favorite song in the show, "Here On Who". But that's okay. That means we're closer to my solos.

I wait in the band room, listening to the show on the speaker one of the parents set up for us. Foster and Kristina sound great as Mr. and Mrs. Mayor, and the Whos – mostly inexperienced middle schoolers – do their best to spit out lots of consonants, in unison, to tell the story of Whoville, no small task.

The action stays in Whoville for the reprise of "Oh, The Thinks You Can Think", "It's Possible", "How to Raise A Child" and "The Military". Does this Who section ever end? In rehearsals, I hadn't noticed how long this part went on. I've still got ages until I'm back onstage. At least it sounds like Foster is acing Mr. Mayor.

"Alone in the Universe" – Horton's and JoJo's duet – gets a huge round of applause, which is my cue to move into the stage left wing. Finally, we're transitioning back to the jungle. Emily and her ukelele sound fantastic as they begin "The One Feather Tail of Miss Gertrude McFuzz". But no time for admiration. My first big number is coming up. Time to get back into character.

I close my eyes, take a few deep breaths, and remember my damaged Mayzie story. My clique – Bird Girls Lucey, Jocelyn and Aimee – gather behind me. If I weren't about to go onstage, I'd be able to wallow in the irony of Lucey and Jocelyn being my supporting characters. But I have to focus.

We're on. I strut to center stage while the Bird Girls hang back to the side. Gertrude and I start our back and forth. I get through the weaker early lines of "Amayzing Mayzie" by focusing on telling the story, and crescendo into the more musically interesting chorus.

Only onstage can I be this free, confident, brash and colorful. I jerk my hips side to side, and bump out my butt in time with the music, making people laugh. I am swishing my long tail of many feathers when a soft gasp escapes from the audience. What the–? Did I have a wardrobe malfunction or something? While I salsa around with the Bird Girls, I scan my costume. Everything looks okay. I look at the Bird Girls to see if they're sending me any silent signals. Nothing. Must have been my imagination. But

Jocelyn really needs to work on staying in character. She looks way too pissed off for this song. Back to singing.

At the end, I inhale as much air as humanly possible to support my final "me" and let it rip. I sound right on key to me. Hopefully I am. With a flourish of my hands over my head, the final notes of the song play, and we're done. I exit, leaving my posse behind me. I think I like having followers. I definitely like having an audience that claps as long as they can, right up until when Gertrude starts speaking again.

We stay in Nool for the rest of Act One. Gertrude eats sketchy pills to grow a fabulous tail in hopes of attracting Horton. The Wickersham Brothers, a thinly veiled bad boy gang of bullies, torment Horton, stealing his clover-speck and giving it to Vlad Vladikoff, the eagle, who flies off with it and lets it go mid-air. In the middle of Horton and the Whos freaking out that the clover is falling, the Cat freezes the action. In our case, this means lights down on the stage except one spotlight on Lindsay. The audience loves it as he breaks the fourth wall and sings to them "How Lucky You Are".

When Lindsay yells "curtain", nothing happens. I don't know if it's always staged this way, but Ms. English uses this line for a real curtain closing, so we can get the egg/nest/tree and other props onstage for the next scene while Horton continues his speck search in front of the curtain. So where the heck is the curtain? "Curtain," Lindsay says again, with an exaggerated motion toward stage right where the curtain pulley is located. The audience laughs. When he says it a third time, the audience knows it's a mistake and their guffaws are replaced by nervous laughter that trickles away.

From offstage, I can see Lindsay trying to think of ways to improvise. He folds his arms, looks up and whistles. He pretends to tap dance. I see Mr. Kent being pushed toward the curtain pulley by Mrs. Carter. Adrienne is in the stage left wing with me, and I don't even have to look to know she's fuming. I can feel the waves of frustration rolling off my usually chill friend.

The curtain finally closed, I walk calmly to center stage and climb onto my nest. Soon, the curtain re-opens and Emily/Gertrude comes on for "Notice Me, Horton". It's a beautiful lament. In fact, *Seussical* is full of beautiful ballads, like "Alone In the Universe" and my favorite, "Solla Sollew". But no time to sink into sentimentality now, because it's time for another dose of Mayzie sass in my reprise of "How Lucky You Are".

My confessional is a blast to sing, partly because I'm playing off of Lindsay as the Cat and Ben as Horton, and our timing is perfect, if I say so myself. Admitting to popping pills in "Amayzing Mayzie" was bad enough. Now, I'm talking about my affair with a night owl who got me pregnant and left me. I am bored, I am self-centered, I am persecuted. I scheme as I sing. I convince Horton to sit on my egg and blow out of there, free at last.

Like Mayzie if she were real, I feel a twinge of regret as I walk away, but tell myself it's for the best. Horton will be a much better mother than I could ever be.

Things may be resolved for Mayzie, sort of, but for the other main characters, they're looking pretty bleak. As I watch from the wing, the Bird Girls explain much of the narrative in song and for once, their harmonies don't give me chills. I must be getting used to them. The freezing cold Horton, grounded-because-she-can't-fly-with-her-huge-tail Gertrude, battered-from-falling-through-the-air JoJo and Whos, campily sing how lucky they are, and the Cat in the Hat sends the audience off for intermission.

    End Act I.

CHAPTER 29: INTERMISSION

$\mathcal{A}$s I walked down the hallway behind the stage, Adrienne popped around the corner and motioned me frantically to follow her. We stopped outside the computer room door, which was shut most of the way.

"Don't you ever, ever, pull a stunt like that again, or you will be kicked out of this program forever. Do you understand me?"

Holy crap! It was Ms. English. Who was she talking to, I asked Adrienne with my eyes.

She put her index finger to her lips and then in the air to say listen.

"Me? Why me?" It was Jocelyn. "She's the one who started it! I didn't do anything."

"Jocelyn, you grabbed her arm onstage! And almost pulled her off her feet! That was totally unprofessional. The whole audience noticed. Didn't you hear them gasping?"

Ohhh.

"I'll yank you from the show right now unless you apologize to me and Lucey. We can get by with one less Bird Girl, you know." Pause. "Now." I got that creepily satisfying glow you get when someone who's not you is getting reamed out.

"I'm sorry," Jocelyn said quietly and clearly unwillingly.

"Apology accepted," said Lucey in a tone that made me picture her smug face. "Can I go now? I really have to pee and it takes forever with this leotard."

"Not so fast. Jocelyn, you can go if you want." Adrienne and I looked around for a place to hide but of course there wasn't one. We were in a hallway. But Jocelyn didn't come out. She wouldn't want to miss the fun, after all. Adrienne and I resumed our casual, we're-not-listening poses.

"You, Lucey, are in just as much trouble. You've been pulling focus from the other Bird Girls all night, and I know you even tried to upstage Sadie. I don't blame Jocelyn for trying to pull you back," Ms. English said. "Not that that excuses what you did," she said, turning to Jocelyn probably. "But it stops now. I'm sick of it. We're all sick of it."

"Yeah," Jocelyn said, defensively.

Silence. I pictured Ms. English giving Jocelyn the evil eye.

"You are part of a trio of birds, and part of a cast. An ensemble. That means you work together. You are not the star, Lucey. And acting like this, you're guaranteeing that you never will be. At least not as long as I'm director."

A fake sniffle from inside. Oh please, don't tell me she's pretending to cry.

"In Act Two, you will stay in your place. No stepping in front of Jocelyn and Aimee. No singing louder than the others – make your voice mesh or don't sing at all. And no speaking Sadie's lines with her."

What the eff?

"Got it?" Pause. "I didn't hear you. Do you understand me, Lucey? I'm perfectly happy to let Aimee have a Bird Gird solo if you two don't shape up."

"But the harmonies! You need more than Aimee for the–"

"Eh! Quiet! All I want to hear out of your mouth right now is that you understand."

Pause. Man, Lucey didn't give in easily.

"I understand. And I'll do it the way you want, if you think it's best for the show that I contain my talent." How did she brown-nose and brag at the same time?

"I think it's best." I heard a suppressed laugh in Ms. English's voice. "Now apologize, Lucey. We're waiting."

Adrienne and I broke into huge grins, visualizing Lucey's torment.

Finally, we heard a huge sigh. "Fine. I'm sorry. Can we get on with the show now? And I really need to pee." A chair scraped across the linoleum floor. Adrienne and I quickly walked down the hallway, our giggles getting louder as we got farther away.

Safe in a corner of the art room, Adrienne fiddled with her hair and stared at the floor.

"Adrienne, what did she mean about Lucey saying my lines? Was she really doing that?"

She looked up like she was surprised I was still there.

"Oh, yeah, she was mouthing your words whenever you spoke, and once or twice I think I could actually hear her."

"No way! And what exactly did Jocelyn do during 'Amayzing Mayzie'?"

Adrienne sighed. "Lucey kept stepping in front of Jocelyn and Aimee, like she was the lead Bird Girl or something, so Jocelyn tried to pull her back."

"Are you effing kidding me? We're in a show for God's sake. Don't they have any respect for the theatre? Adrienne? Hey, what's up?"

"No offense, but Lucey trying to steal focus from you is only one of our problems. And Ms. English just fixed that. This show sucks! Haven't you noticed all of the mistakes backstage?"

"No, sorry," I shrugged. "What were they?"

"The parents have missed like five cues. Scene changes are taking way too long. They totally missed the curtain closing after 'It's Possible'. We had to pull the bathtub off in front of everyone."

"Yeah, I caught that one," I said, trying to act pissed off, but honestly I was still processing the Lucey/Jocelyn episode and wondering how badly it upstaged my big solo. And absorbing the satisfaction of them being yelled at by the director.

"And they're not using the prop list I made. And they're running around like chickens with their heads cut off. Mrs. Carter is the worst, whispering left and right, pushing people here and there. It's horrible."

"Is that why you're working stage left this year?"

"Yup. To stay away from them. I even ditched Tom over there. He said he'd stay to make sure they didn't mess up anything too much. There's not as much action over here but at least I can be in charge of this small part of the show." My poor friend was close to tears. "This has been the worst opening night ever!"

"Oh, Ade, I'm sorry. That stinks." I put my arm around her shoulder. "I guess it hasn't been very smooth, has it?" It felt really weird to not be as upset as Adrienne. Theatre was my life, after all. I think my euphoria from playing Mayzie well in Act One, despite Lucey's attempts to upstage me, was making me care less about the small things. Or maybe watching Mrs. Holman battle tuberculosis put our little show with its politics and drama into perspective. Or maybe the overwhelming relief I felt having survived coming clean with my dad was insulating me from show concerns. Whatever the reason, I was calm and I was going with it.

"Guys, come on," Foster yelled at us from the hallway. "Ms. English wants everyone in the band room, stat."

"*O*kay, gather round," Ms. English said, the chatter of six or seven small groups dying quickly as we formed a circle around our director.

"Just a few notes, then I'll save the rest for tomorrow. Stop talking with your mikes on! I heard someone say, 'I hate this number' from backstage. Really? Really? If you're wearing a mike, assume it's on all the time. If you really need to talk, have someone check to make sure the red light is on and the mike is off.

"At another point, it was quiet onstage and I heard the cast whispering in the wings. Not acceptable, you guys! I don't want to hear anything, from anybody, unless you're onstage.

"Number three – how many times have I said, if you're in the wings and you can see the audience, then they can see you too? There's nothing worse than an offstage character distracting the audience. It ruins the magic.

"Honestly, it's like some of you have never done a show before."

"That's probably because some of them *have* never done a show before," Kristina said grumpily, nodding toward a clump of seventh-graders.

"Okay, so let's get focused for Act Two–"

Lindsay cleared his throat loudly and dramatically. "Oh, fearless director, don't you have another note for hmmm," he said, folding his cat arms over his tuxedoed chest, and pointing one white-gloved finger at Jimmy while looking the other way.

Ms. English focused on Jimmy, who was horsing around with the other monkeys. "Jimmy! Where *were* you? Pay attention. Do not miss that cue tomorrow. And it's not funny!" she reprimanded as the three monkeys laughed.

"Okay, that's all for now. Places for Act Two. Let's do it like it's the last time!"

CHAPTER 30: ACT TWO

I should be waiting in the band room because I'm not on for a while, but I'm peeking from stage left as Lindsay strides to center stage with the house lights still up. A few kids spy him and laugh and yell to their parents. The Cat clears his throat loudly and dramatically, like in the band room minutes before. The house lights dim and the spotlight focuses on the Cat, who begins his manic conducting of the entr'acte. He puts on a serious conductor face, he plays air guitar, he acts surprised when the piano makes a loud crash, he even struts like Mick Jagger, making the older members of the audience chuckle.

Why is one person allowed to have so much talent? Lindsay is so funny and such a good actor, on top of being a star athlete not to mention one of the hottest guys in school. It seems a little unfair. But I have to give him props for putting in the time, in the end, to perfect his performance. Every second of the musical introduction to Act Two is choreographed, and I'm pretty sure Lindsay came up with all of it on his own. If only he had done it a month ago and saved us all the aggravation of wondering if he'd be ready by show time.

Horton the Elephant is captured by hunters and sold at auction to a man from the circus. Lindsay breaks the fourth wall again to engage the audience in the auction. At first, I can tell people don't understand what to do. But it's Friday night and a lot of students are in the audience. They catch on quickly, yelling out bids for the elephant that quickly get silly. "Ten million dollars." "Fifty cents and a cup of coffee." "I'll give you twenty dollars and Principal Zowicki." Before he loses control, Lindsay returns to the script to end the auction, ignoring a few final bids hollered out by enthusiastic students.

Since we're not doing "The Circus McGurkus", "Egg, Nest & Tree" leads to the second, short reprise of "How Lucky You Are" as Ben/Horton pleads for me to come back and take my egg. Then on to my second favorite number, "Mayzie in Palm Beach". No introductory dialogue – it's right into the song.

As I sing about my carefree life, Lindsay plays the Cat in the Hat playing a pool boy serving my bathing bird a cocktail in the Florida sun. He cracks me up with his interjections about how lucky I am – *Seussical* gets a lot of mileage from the how lucky theme – but I'm so deep into Mayzie it's easy to stay in character. As the Cat fans me with a fake palm frond, I switch to whining mode, looking for something new and interesting to do. The Cat holds out his two hands to me, as if they're holding a piece of paper top and bottom, but in between those hands? Air. Nothing but air. He doesn't have the circus flyer prop.

I recover quickly, taking the pretend flyer from his hands and proclaiming my sudden interest in attending the circus. I step into the stage left wing and almost bump into Adrienne in the dark. "No flyer!" she hisses, handing me a red-and-white-striped popcorn container. I immediately go back onstage to ponder Horton sitting on my egg in a nest in a tree.

We Seuss-speak a bit and I break into "Amayzing Horton", my favorite song in the whole show. I get to change emotions on a dime in this one, from fear of hatching my own egg to pretend admiration of Horton's parenting skills to mock contrition, to the climax of dramatic, condescending gratitude. The audience laughs and I get goosebumps mid-song. And then, a touch of sincerity for the last few lines, and I do it. I escape from my egg for the last time.

I'm done. I tear up and I'm not sure if it's because I'm internalizing Mayzie's regret or because my lines are over and there's still half an hour left in the show.

I stay in the wing, facing the stage, back just far enough that I can't see the audience. Ben knocks his short reprise of "Alone in the Universe" out of the park. His wooden acting skills don't seem to matter much in this show, since most of the lines are sung and he's got a great voice. With perfect pitch, he makes the segue from the reprise into the "Solla Sollew" introduction with the word *lullaby*, the sweetest change in the entire show.

As "Solla Sollew" starts, I wish we had an actual band or even a boom box with the full score being played, because great as Patrick is on the piano, this ballad needs lush strings and a haunting flute. But as Ben keeps singing, I forget about the instruments and get carried away by the singing. When the circus animals join Ben on the chorus, I sing too, from the wings. Adrienne hums next to me.

Man, this song is beautiful. As it builds, Mr. and Mrs. Mayor and JoJo walk on, staying apart from the jungle characters and singing along. The first time Ben, Foster, Kristina and Max sing a line together, I almost cry right there. It's unbelievably sad.

As we start the final chorus, repeating *solla sollew* over and over, I notice how still the audience is, even though the only action onstage is a small group of people singing the same words again and again. Nothing else. And it is hypnotizing. The simple harmonies are gorgeous, the audience cares about our characters, and they are mesmerized.

I get little shivers all the time when I hear pretty music, but when Ben sings his final "with you", a shudder of unidentifiable emotion runs all the way from my shoulders to my toes.

As the applause builds and recedes, and I turn to go to the band room, I realize Adrienne is holding my hand. I give her a big smile, detach and go.

With the applause dying, the general and cadets stomp on, their chants shattering the "Solla Sollew" mood as they march into "Green Eggs and Ham II".

In the band room, I sit next to Emily on a cold, beige folding chair.

"My tail okay?" she asks, peering over her shoulder at her short Gertrude tail, the one she started the show with. It's basically a blue feather duster minus the handle, plucked to death to look skimpy and sad.

I check our mike buttons to be sure they're off. "Looks fine. My make-up?"

"Looks fine."

We sit quietly and listen for a while. When the Cat advises JoJo to follow his instincts and think for himself, Emily jumps up. "Gotta go," she says as she leaves the band room, straightening her big round prop glasses, taped across the bridge Harry Potter style.

While she sings "All For You", I check my make-up in the bathroom. Soon after I get back, the Wickersham monkeys – including Jimmy this time – and the Sour Kangaroo are arresting Horton and taking him to trial.

"The People Versus Horton the Elephant" is crazily chaotic and fun, filled with the usual amount of *Seussical* tempo changes. You know the rest. With the jungle creatures wanting to destroy the speck and every Who they don't believe is on it, JoJo finally makes himself heard by inventing a new word that breaks through the who-o-sphere and is heard in the jungle. Horton is redeemed. The Whos are safe.

When we break into the finale, "Oh, The Thinks You Can Think", I have to sing from offstage since Mayzie is still in self-inflicted exile. During rehearsals, I thought about asking Ms. English if I could be in this scene, since it's the finale and you could argue not part of the story line. In the end, I tried to be professional, and settled for singing from the sidelines.

It's an all-out party on the stage. I lean forward enough to see a slice of the audience and everyone is smiling and nodding their head or moving their shoulders in time to the music, infected with Seuss-itis. The Whos and Jungle of Nool characters storm off stage and get ready for bows. Foster picks me up around the waist and whirls me around, making me kick Lucey by accident. She glares but I don't care. She goes on for her curtain call way before me.

"Green Eggs and Ham" plays as we stream back onstage and take turns moving downstage for bows, first the Whos and Nools in groups, then the Wickershams together and the Bird Girls together, then the individual stars. I am fifth from last, with only JoJo, Gertrude, Horton and the Cat after me. The audience roars when I take my bow. Oh yeah. Did I mention I love this show?

(Blackout. Curtains close. END OF PLAY.)

CHAPTER 31: UNSCRIPTED

$\mathcal{M}$om turned to face me and Alex in the back seat of the car.

"That was the best show you've ever done, honey, I'm so proud of you." She'd already told me this in the school lobby, but knowing Mom, she would say it about ten more times before she'd feel the message was delivered.

"Thanks, Mom," I said, not unhappy to hear her say it again. This time anyway.

"Alex, wasn't she great?"

Alex looked at me uncertainly.

"It's okay to say she was great. Sadie must have told you John and I know you two are still dating. The cat's out of the bag. So we can all start acting normally again."

"Well, normally might be a stretch for Sadie," Alex said, grinning, his shoulders relaxing.

"Whoa ho," Dad said from the driver's seat. "Careful, Alex, or you won't be dating much longer." He grinned, too. In fact, all four of us were smiling. I guess ending the charade was a relief to everyone. "Now listen, kids, just because we know doesn't mean the rules of disengagement have changed. No going into each other's rooms–"

"John, stop it. Not now. We can trust Alex to follow the rules. Let's deal with this later and just enjoy the – Sadie, what do you always call it? – the post-show high."

I scrunched up my forehead. "What do you mean, 'we can trust Alex'? Don't you think you can trust me, too?"

"Of course, Sadie, that's not what I meant." She turned back to face the road. "Let's de-brief the show," she said, every bit the PR executive. "What was that bit with Jocelyn Meyer and Lucey Landau? That wasn't in the script, was it?"

"Ho ho," Dad said again. Wow, he was in a jolly mood. "I doubt it. Looked like we were gonna have an all-out cat fight for a minute."

"Yeah, that was pretty pathetic, wasn't it? Leave it to Lucey to mess up my big solo."

"It wasn't that noticeable, Sade. I didn't even see it happening," Alex said, daring to take my hand. "I only heard about it after."

"That's because you couldn't take your eyes off my daughter," Dad said, looking in the rearview mirror. "You probably wouldn't have noticed if a real elephant walked onto the stage and sat on that egg. Of course, in that skimpy costume..." He stopped talking, his cheerful face turning somber.

"Anyway," Mom said, dragging out the syllables, "I think all you kids did a wonderful job with the show. No offense to Mr. Ellison, but I think having a real director is going to be good for your theatre program."

"Yeah, except that it's over. That was our last CDC show," I said. I wished she hadn't brought this up. I didn't want to ruin tonight's glow by thinking about the fact that CDC was basically over for me now.

Alex tightened his grip on my hand until I looked at him. "That's okay, because you've got two more performances, and then there are going to be lots of other cool shows in your life."

*M*om knew it took me a few hours to come down off a post-show high before I could sleep. Surprisingly, she left me and Alex on the living room couch and went to bed.

"They're being so cool about this now. Do you think we could have told them sooner and saved ourselves all the aggravation?" I asked.

Alex smirked. "Are you kidding? Your Dad is still freaked out at the thought of us being in the same house, can't you tell? If we'd told them sooner, I'd have been packed off somewhere else for sure. Even your parents aren't that nice. But my mom will be home Sunday after the show, so I think as long as we're good, they'll be okay with me being here 'til then."

"Plus, Jesse comes home for winter break tomorrow, so you'll have to move to the couch anyway. Something tells me they'll be happier with us on different floors. And if you decide to visit Jesse in the middle of the night, well I hear his door doesn't squeak anymore."

We laughed and he put his arm around me. "At least now we can do this," Alex said, snuggling up closer.

"Yeah, as long as my dad's not watching," I said, still laughing.

"He doesn't have a shotgun hiding anywhere, does he?"

I put my head on his shoulder and closed my eyes, rewinding the tape in my head from tonight's performance to re-play two or three times before sleeping. Even with Lucey's interference, I pulled it off. Based on the congratulations I got from people I didn't even know after the show, my Mayzie was a hit.

Alex knew I was thinking about the show. "Hey," he said softly. "Did I tell you yet how great you were as Mayzie? Not to mention beautiful and really, really sexy."

"Shhh," I said, smiling in thanks.

"Oh, sorry, go ahead. Play your tape." He leaned into me and shut his eyes.

Our performances Saturday night and Sunday afternoon were practically perfect, and our biggest crowds ever packed the auditorium. Dr. Seuss brought out the families in droves. The only mishap was on Sunday, when the cord connecting Emily's mike to the battery pack got caught in her feathers when she switched from her regular tail to her out-of-control, trying-to-impress-Horton one.

Backstage, the stage crew drama settled down because Ms. English realized Mrs. Carter was constantly re-assigning parent volunteer roles opening night, creating mayhem and disorganization. She stepped in and told the parents they would have the same roles – moving the same set pieces at the same point in each show – for the final two performances.

"But that will be boring for them," objected Mrs. Carter. "I'm merely trying to keep it interesting."

"Actually, I think it will be reassuring for them," countered Ms. English. "Then they won't have to wonder what they're supposed to be doing when. They'll just know."

And Ms. English had taken Adrienne's prop list to Mr. Fishbein, giving him personal responsibility for getting the stage right props in place before the show and during intermission.

Still, Adrienne stayed on the stage left side for the weekend shows, joking it was safer over there. I knew how much she missed running stage crew, which totally sucked since this was our last show and she wouldn't have another chance.

After Sunday's show, before I could break into my usual post-run tears, I rushed into the school lobby in full make-up and costume to find Alex and his mom.

"Alex!" I threw my arms around him. He stiffened, scanning the crowd of people mingling in the lobby.

"Oh yeah, it's okay," he reminded himself. "It's going to take a while to feel normal again, isn't it?" He grinned and handed me a small bouquet of daisies and yellow roses. "Here, these are for you."

Finally, I could associate with my boyfriend, and have him give me flowers, with people watching. "You shouldn't have! But thanks, they're beautiful." I stuck my nose into a rose and inhaled. "Where's your mom?"

"I left her sitting in the auditorium for now. I thought it might be too crazy for her out here since she's still kind of weak." Ben bumped into him and bounced through the throng of people like a pinball, proving Alex's point.

"Can we go say hi to her? You told her about us, right?"

He opened the auditorium door and waited for me to go through.

"Told her? Who do you think listened to me complain about our situation the past few months? She's known all along."

After a quick visit with Alex's mom, who looked better than she had in months, we moved toward the auditorium door, Alex and Mrs. Holman putting on their jackets as they walked.

"Mom, put your sweater on too. It's cold out," Alex said.

Mrs. Holman shook her head. "I'm fine with my jacket. Fresh air feels so good after weeks of stale hospital air." She held her peach sweater firmly in front of her.

He frowned but really couldn't be unhappy with her. "Okay, fine then, let's take you home. Finally!" Alex said, twirling the car keys around his index finger and smiling.

"Not so fast," Crudup Police Chief Wyatt said, suddenly blocking the doorway with his black-clad, six-foot frame.

Oh my God, did he really just say that? And where did he come from? It was so cliché I wanted to laugh, but the seriousness in his voice glued my mouth shut.

"Jenny Holman, you're under arrest for the theft of five hundred pills of oxycodone from the hospital pharmacy." All desire to laugh evaporated. He held out handcuffs. "Sorry to ruin your homecoming." I could feel the few people lingering in the auditorium turn to watch us.

"What are you talking about?" Alex exclaimed, stepping between the chief and his mother. "We've already done this, remember? And she was cleared. You didn't even have any real evidence."

I flashed back to the first time Mrs. Holman was arrested, amazed at how much older Alex seemed this time around.

"Mrs. Holman?" the chief said, stepping to the side and looking at her as if she were the only one in the room.

"Alex, it's okay. Let him take me," Mrs. Holman said softly.

Alex stared at his mother, eyes wide.

"Why? This is a mistake, isn't it? Mom?"

"Alex." Her voice broke. "Alex," she started again, "I'm so sorry." She looked up at her six-foot son and put her hand on his shoulder, crying. "I'm so sorry, I'm so sorry," she repeated, tears quickly flooding the wrinkles around her eyes.

"What are you talking about? You're not saying you did it, are you?" Alex's voice was getting firmer, as if he could will the right answer out of her. "You didn't do it!"

Mrs. Holman swallowed. "I never said that, exactly. It's complicated, honey. The truth is–" She looked down at her hands, which twisted her sweater mercilessly. "The truth is, I did take the pills."

CHAPTER 32: LIFELINE

"Alex, please talk to me," I implored, but he wouldn't look at me. I couldn't really blame him. His mother was a thief. She'd admitted it. Turns out the hospital security camera had caught her in the act. The police had held back that information, hoping Mrs. Holman would relax and lead them to her buyer. They were after bigger fish than her. But apparently they were sick of waiting and decided public embarrassment might be better incentive to get her to reveal who she sold the drugs to.

They had taken her from the school in a cruiser, lights flashing, while everyone watched. Their unnecessary flair for the dramatic pissed me off. Why couldn't they have arrested her at home? I couldn't imagine what Alex was feeling, but I couldn't get him to talk.

He'd squealed out of the school parking lot alone, leaving me to ride with my parents. By the time we got home, he was sitting on my front steps tying his sneakers, his face a hard, grim mask. He yanked the lace on his right shoe so hard it broke.

"Screw it," he grumbled, standing up and running off, the broken lace flapping helplessly.

And that was the last thing he'd said to me in three days. We entered another alternate universe. We should have been back to normal: Alex and his mother in their own home, he and I officially dating again, everything in its proper place. Instead, I could barely reach him, literally or figuratively. Even though his mother was in jail, he moved back home and my parents didn't even try to stop him. At least that's where I think he went. For all I knew, he was cruising the streets night and day and not sleeping anywhere. He wouldn't return my calls or texts, he didn't go to school, and when I knocked on his door, he pretended not to be home.

Mom and Dad said to give him time, but I knew they were worried too.

$\mathcal{F}$inally, Wednesday after school, he was standing in his front doorway when I got off the school bus. I walked up his path, feeling like a million years had passed since we were in these exact same positions at the end of the summer.

Silently, he opened the door. He wore wrinkled clothes and a few days stubble. Taking my hand, he led me to his old blue couch. He moved to sit, but I held him up.

"Alex," I said, and wrapped my arms around his torso, trying to envelop him as if he were a baby.

He hugged back tightly, gave one extra forceful squeeze, and separated from me.

"I'm okay. In case you were worried."

"Of course I was worried! I'm still worried."

"Well, you don't need to be." He eased onto the couch, pulling me down next to him. "I've been figuring everything out. Obviously I can't count on my mother anymore, like my father and my brother. But I can move back here in a few weeks when I turn eighteen, as long as I make enough at my job to pay for it. So I'll probably have to quit basketball–"

"Alex. Alex, please stop. I mean, it's great that you're figuring everything out, but maybe you're going too fast. You don't even know what's going to happen to your mom. Maybe she'll be back soon."

His face relaxed for a second, and in that second I saw how exhausted he was. Quickly, the hard, focused look was back.

"I can't plan on that. I have to take care of myself."

"Hey." I grabbed his hand and squeezed it. "I know this is really weird, and I guess you're feeling let down. Disappointed. Something. But have you even talked to her?"

He shook his head.

"You have to hear her side of the story, Alex. You know she's not like your father. She loves you, and would never hurt you on purpose. Don't give up on her. You can't."

He scrunched up his mouth as if in pain. "Whatever. We'll see."

"And hey, you have me. You'll always have me." I squeezed his hand again, knowing as I spoke that I might be lying. I loved Alex and always would, but neither one of us knew what the next few years would bring. At that moment, I decided our future was, at least partly, in our control. And I committed right then to always having Alex in my life, somehow, some way.

"One way or another," I said with more conviction, "we will always have each other. Right?"

He closed his eyes and nodded. He opened them and fixed his sea-green eyes on my mud-brown ones, connecting us soul to soul. "Right." He stared as if seeing me for the first time since I walked in. Leaning forward, he kissed me, a mature kiss, slow and certain. We sighed in unison.

Alex finally talked to his mother, who was being held in the Dayton Correctional Facility. She'd basically confessed, so there was no bail or time at home. Mrs. Holman stole out of desperation. The restaurant where she worked her second job had been slow for months, and she was falling behind on her bills. She was heart-broken at the thought of Alex not being able to afford college. So when a friend of a friend asked if she could get some prescription drugs from the hospital, she said yes.

The judge let her off light – three months in a minimum-security prison – since it was her first offense, she wasn't a drug user herself, and her son depended on her income. She panicked at first about how Alex would get by for those three months, but my parents and Alex's aunt and uncle in California convinced her he would be taken care of. He would stay with us a few more weeks until he turned eighteen in January, and then they would support him after he moved back home.

They also convinced Alex that he should continue with basketball instead of quitting and taking a job, since a sports scholarship was probably his best bet for getting into college. That made me very happy because it meant maybe he and I could get back to our regularly scheduled life and salvage what was left of senior year.

Getting back to normal was harder than Alex and I thought it would be, mainly because we didn't even know what that meant anymore. He kept sleeping across the hall from me. Was that normal or not? We were officially, publicly and privately dating again. That should have felt normal but after months of pretending, it just felt weird. His mom was healthy again, but in jail. That was definitely not normal.

And I experienced the most devastating case of post-show letdown in history, having performed in my last high school show, ever. Mrs. Holman's arrest right after the last show hadn't interrupted or slowed the onset of my PSL. It just added a touch of the surreal to an already disorienting condition. Foster, Kristina and Adrienne were suffering, too. We tried commiserating our way out of our bad moods, but that only made it worse.

So we were a sullen bunch of seniors in the auditorium the Friday before Christmas vacation, when Ms. English called a special CDC meeting.

"Thanks for coming to our last CDC meeting of the year," Ms. English said as Lindsay bombed down the aisle and slammed into a seat with a bang.

"You mean of our lives," grumbled Foster, slumping down in the seat next to me.

"Well, maybe not." Fos and I shifted up an inch at the same time. "That's why I called this meeting."

For once, no one interrupted. No questions. No guesses. This was too important.

"As you know, Crudup will not have a spring play. Instead, the music department is sponsoring a talent show. However, we've been asked to participate in a show at the Academy of Dance and Music in Sutton." Everyone sat up straight now, hanging on her every word. "I need to let them know this week if we have enough students to do it. So, who's interested?"

The floodgates opened. Foster, Kristina, Lucey and I started asking questions at the same time, talking over each other. The others including Ben, Aimee and Jocelyn, murmured to each other while Lindsay sat there, watching and laughing.

"Okay, okay," Ms. English said, holding up both palms like she was at gunpoint. "I gather there's interest. I thought there would be. That's why I went after this opportunity when I heard we couldn't have a spring play."

I liked this woman. Like Mr. Ellison, she was totally in our corner. And she sang, danced and acted.

"This is the deal. ADAM – that's what they call it – wants to do something special for their musical this year. They have plenty of dancers and musicians, but no acting program yet, so they need to collaborate with another school. And they chose us. The director of the school heard about your original shows from last year, and thought we would make a good partner since there might be an original element to their show."

We sat, absorbing her words.

"What's the show?" Three of us broke the silence with the same question.

Ms. English laughed. "I can't say yet. They're not even positive yet. But trust me, it's going to be great."

My chest heaved with relief and anticipation. A new lease on life. I was so happy I wanted to cry.

Why, when it was senior year and I wanted more than ever to freeze my high school experiences in my memory, was it so hard to hang onto anything? I wanted to capture every class, every assembly, every bad lunch and, most of all, every spontaneous, hysterical moment with my friends, and store them in my brain for safekeeping. I wanted to remember every sight, sound and smell, forever.

It scared me how fast it was all going.

You'd of thought that with my college applications done, I'd be daydreaming about my future at one of those colleges, but I was fixated on the present. I kept catching myself choking up at something simple, like Adrienne and Tom holding hands. Or Lindsay's backtalk in class. Or Big Jason's jabs rolling off Foster like water off a duck's back. I wouldn't have Adrienne next year. I wouldn't have Foster next year. I wouldn't have any of my friends. I might even miss Jason.

Nostalgia slunk into my life, unbidden.

I was even sad about experiences I hadn't had, like the Homecoming Dance, and having a boyfriend senior year, or I should say *acting* like I had a boyfriend senior year. I didn't talk about my feelings with Alex, because his mother hadn't even seen him play in the state soccer championship, and now she wasn't going to see any of his basketball games. Obviously, I couldn't complain to him.

At least I had one more high school play to look forward to, even though it wouldn't be on the Crudup stage. That kept me from slipping into an all-out, full-force, nostalgia-fueled thespian depression.

But there would be no more high school soccer games. No more Halloween-themed Spirit Weeks. No more fall report cards, or winter exams. No more Harvest Bonfires or horrible Christmas meals in the caf. No more lame holiday decorations in the Crudup lobby.

It was all over. My last fall semester of high school was done.

I had no idea how to script the rest.


```
(Blackout. Curtains close. End of Sadie's Senior
Year, Act I.)
```

ACKNOWLEDGEMENTS

As always, thanks to Gabby and Natalie for their invaluable critique, which just gets better with age. Thanks to my other reviewers, Mom, Joan and Kathleen. I want to acknowledge Sarah Richards of StageLeft Productions in Central Massachusetts. My portrayal of *Seussical* is based on her vision. Thanks also to Chelsea Cipolla of My College Audition, Rhode Island College alumnus Jenna Tremblay, and Joel Brandwine of Boston University, for their insights about college theatre programs. And, of course, thanks to Dr. Seuss, *Seussical* composer and librettist Stephen Flaherty, and *Seussical* lyricist and librettist Lynn Ahrens, for creating works that continue to inspire new generations and new iterations of their fantastic stories and songs.

ABOUT THE AUTHOR

Theatre-loving S.M. Stevens performed in and worked backstage at numerous high school, college and community theatre productions, but she never got the lead. She grew up in Maine, was involved in the drama programs at Cornell University and the University of Southern Maine, and lives in Central Massachusetts.

She hopes the Bit Players series will fill the void of fiction for musical theatre-lovers, and introduce newcomers to the special world of theatre.

Visit www.BitPlayers.me for book and theatre news, and links to theatre organizations. (That's .me not .com.) Visit the Bit Players Pinterest page for visual ideas on costumes, makeup, sets and props for your next production.

Made in the USA
Charleston, SC
17 February 2014